SAILING TIME'S OCEAN

by

Terence M. Green

Afterword by

Robert J. Sawyer

Robert J.
SAWYER
B O O K S

Robert J. Sawyer Books are published by Red Deer Press, A Fitzhenry & Whiteside Company
1512, 1800–4 Street S.W., Calgary Alberta Canada T2S 2S5
www. robertjsawyerbooks.com • www.reddeerpress.com

Library and Archives Canada Cataloguing in Publication
Green, Terence M
[Children of the rainbow]
Sailing time's ocean / Terence M. Green ; afterword by Robert J. Sawyer.
First published: Toronto : McClelland & Stewart, 1992 under title:
Children of the rainbow .
ISBN 0-88995-357-0
I. Title. II. Title: Children of the rainbow.
PS8563.R41685C46 2006   C813'.54   C2006-903252-1

U.S. Publisher Cataloging-in-Publication Data (Library of Congress Standards)
Green, Terence M.
 Sailing time's ocean / Terence M. Green ; afterword by Robert J. Sawyer.
Rev. ed. of: Children of the Rainbow ; Toronto : McClelland & Stewart, 1992.
[256] p. : cm.
ISBN 0-88995-357-0 (pbk.)
1. Fantasy. I. Sawyer, Robert J. II. Title.
813.54 dc22   PR9199.3.G7574C48 2006

Credits   Edited for the Press by Robert J. Sawyer
                 Cover and text design by Karen (Petherick) Thomas
                 Cover image courtesy Firstlight Images
                 Printed and bound in Canada by Friesens for Red Deer Press

Acknowledgments Financial support provided by the Canada Council, the
                 Government of Canada through the Book Publishing Industry
                 Development Program (BPIDP).

Canada Council   Conseil des Arts
for the Arts   du Canada

DEDICATION

For Merle. Again. Always.

ACKNOWLEDGMENTS

A book's genesis is always a wonder, most especially in hindsight. People who helped along the way, who appear in my memory as signposts on this unique journey, include Andrew Weiner, Robert J. Sawyer, Sharon Jarvis, Joan Winston, Laurie Feigenbaum, Ken Luginbuhl, Alex Rade, Lorna Toolis, Bill Hushion, James Adams, Valerie Jacobs, Douglas Gibson, Conor, Owen, Merle, and the entire East York C.I. library staff. Linda Williams of McClelland & Stewart brought enthusiasm and editorial excellence to the manuscript, and the book grew stronger with her help.

The historical facts surrounding *Greenpeace III* and the nuclear testing in the South Pacific, Norfolk Island, the mutiny on the Bounty, and Pitcairn Island are all a matter of fully-documented public record, available to anyone who cares to research them. I have been faithful to that record.

I would also like to acknowledge, with real fondness, a certain third-floor apartment on Heath Street East in Toronto where most of this novel was written. The place shaped this book, and me, in more ways than I can imagine.

Old saws: time changes everything; timing is everything.

Some history…

Children of the Rainbow, originally issued in 1992 by McClelland & Stewart, was, at the time, a signal event: an SF novel published as a mainstream book rather than as a genre title by Canada's largest publisher. Their involvement, greeted with much hope, heralded the possibility of a new literary acceptance and distribution for the form in Canada. But, alas, instead of being the seed that flowered into a tradition, it became the sole blossom of its kind, seeing only Canadian publication, and at M&S the decision to continue in this direction was abandoned.

The reasons for this are integral to the business side of writing, rather than the quality of the work – a situation more common than casual observers might suspect. Truth be told, M&S didn't know anything about SF – what it was, how to market it. A few enthusiastic members of the firm (at the acquisition and editorial level) wanted to get into the field, but it was never sufficiently supported at the top, so the book's life was short and its readership never international. Sometimes this is the way the business goes.

So when I received Rob Sawyer's recent unsolicited call saying that he would very much like to reissue the novel under his "Robert J. Sawyer Books" imprint from Fitzhenry & Whiteside, I was delighted, for Rob does indeed know the field, and there is definite support at the top. Fitzhenry & Whiteside has international distribution, so for the first time the novel will be available worldwide, published and promoted by people who know and care about what they are doing in the field.

Time changes everything; timing is everything.

A tradition, some precedents: Robert A. Heinlein's *The Day After Tomorrow* (1949) appeared originally as *Sixth Column* (1941); Cordwainer Smith's *The Boy Who Bought Old Earth*, which appeared in magazine version in 1964 reappeared in book form as *The Planet Buyer* (1964), and eventually combined (some editing and linking additions) with his posthumously published *The Underpeople* (1968) to form *Norstrilia* (1975), the definitive novel of Smith's saga; Alfred Bester's marvelous (and I use the word in its literal meaning of wonderful, extraordinary and improbable as well as excellent, splendid and fine) *The Stars My Destination* (1956) appeared that same year in the U.K. under the title *Tiger! Tiger!* Robert J. Sawyer himself had *Hobson's Choice* (serialized in Analog magazine, 1994-95) transformed into the Nebula Award winning novel *The Terminal Experiment* (1995); finally, Arthur C. Clarke had the opportunity to reissue his 1953 novel *Against the Fall of Night*, and ended up rewriting it as *The City and the Stars* (and as Sir Arthur noted in his 1956 preface, speaking of his readers: "I hope they will grant an author the right to have second thoughts.")

I trust my readers are as generous.

Invited to go over the story and see if there were any changes I'd like to make to the manuscript for this new edition, slowly, surreptitiously, over a period of some months – in the film tradition of the "Director's Cut" — I saw many (small) things that would indeed benefit the novel, the least of which was not, like so many of my predecessors, a new title. So renewed opportunity offers the chance for a new presentation, and suddenly I find myself, along with you, on a new/old voyage, *sailing time's ocean...*

— *Terence M. Green*
2006

I

On the shadows of the Moon
Climbing thro' Night's highest noon;
In Time's Ocean falling drown'd.

—William Blake

For the Sexes: The Gates of Paradise

* * 1 * *

AUCKLAND
28 April, 1972

Finally, thought McTaggart. It's happening. We're going, at last.

The thirty-eight foot ketch *Vega*, renamed *Greenpeace III,* eased out toward Matiamatia Bay as dusk fell and the temperature dropped. Winter was creeping into the South Pacific and the wind that filled the sails was beginning to bite. McTaggart did not notice, though. He'd been waiting too long for this moment, wanting it too badly for the weather to inter-fere with his exhilaration.

The shore disappeared.

"Course east northeast," called Nigel.

McTaggart turned and smiled at him. "A month of this, eh?"

"There are worse ways to spend one's time."

"Don't I know it." Squinting at him through weathered lids, McTaggart added, "Is there anything you'd rather be doing?"

"Not a thing." Nigel paused, savoring the moment. "Not a damn thing."

Radio Hauraki was soft in the background, muffled by the ancient music of ship and sea, suffused by the gray, wintry sky.

McTaggart turned back toward the sea and the night and the horizon.

Flooding his mind were images and memories, both recent and old. He couldn't yet shake the anger and outrage of being harassed by the Kiwis over the trumped-up smuggling charges, of being purposely detained by Customs, courts, and the Marine Department. It had all been new, even astounding, to this Canadian, who, until recently, had eschewed politics in favor of what he thought of as conservative common sense.

But that was all gone now. Gone like his three daughters whom he had lost in his divorce. At the thought of them, a pang of anguish and love shot through him, siphoning up primal longings that often made his own life seem small. And in the tangle of images that hovered in his brain, he knew that there was indeed some ethereal link between his daughters, his precipitous advance toward the age of forty, and his persistent decision to challenge both the sea and the French government.

And the bomb.

It was all ahead.

McTaggart knew that he was operating from the heart, and that a more realistic man would have assessed the enemy in its various guises more carefully. He shrugged. It was not his nature. He was ignorant of the vast political forces that were against him, blind to the monies changing hands between the Conservative government in Wellington and Paris, unaware of the uranium deals between Ottawa and France, and thus naive to the extent to which people might go to try and stop him. Somehow, much of it didn't matter. For, in an abstract way, he knew that the true object of his challenge was himself, as it always must be, and that the externals were manifestations of this, no matter how awesome.

Even Peru had been bought, he knew, by the promise of $60 million US for loan. The Lima government had exposed itself as only another prostitute, willing to sell its integrity and the possible genetic future of its citizenry for cash on demand.

And General de Gaulle would have his nuclear *force de frappe* at all costs.

Out there in the gathering darkness lay the Mururoa Atoll, *le Centre d'Experimentations Nucléaires du Pacifique,* thirty-five hundred miles away. I wonder, thought McTaggart, if I'll be lucky enough to actually see forty?

Like a thoroughbred stretching its reins, in a sensuous display of life and vigor, *Vega,* the new *Greenpeace III,* replete with its crew of two Canadians, two Englishmen, and an Australian, yawed toward the Kermadec Trench and the International Date Line, its modest length and twelve-and-a-half-foot beam representing the inanimate half of the vast synergy between vessel and human spirit that had launched her.

Out there, unseen and lying in wait, was a nuclear bomb. Ten megatons. Two hundred and fifty times the size of the one that had vaporized Hiroshima.

2

CUZCO, PERU
7 June, 2056

Pope Alejandro I, Venezuela's pride, entered the ceremonial chamber slowly and with a display of ritual as elaborate as that of his host. His entourage consisted of two cardinals and three laymen, his usual advisers and security.

The heavy wooden doors shut silently behind them.

Pope Alejandro had expected to see his host seated regally on a throne, in keeping with the trappings so far. He was mildly surprised to see him at the head of a large table in the center of the room—a table that gave the proceedings more the air of a corporate meeting than a meeting between world religious leaders.

Accompanied by three of his confidants, Huascar, the seventy-one-year-old mystic whose name denoted the brilliant red hummingbird whose feathers were used to adorn Incan princes, sat waiting, without expression. Alejandro's presence—here in this room, with him—at last gave him the leap in credibility that he had been waiting for.

The New Inca Church would rise without hindrance now. No longer could the Roman Catholic pontiff dismiss it as a cult. Huascar saw the Pope's stranglehold on South America open wide in his mind's eye, saw the natural legacy of the Incas resume its rightful place in history, felt the restoration of a heritage that would lead all people into proper communion with nature and its gods.

For the Pope, too, believed.

That was why he was here.

Alejandro's coffee was strong and rich. Across the table, Huascar, resplendent in a cream robe and ornate gold necklace, the white hair a shocking contrast with his bronzed face, stared with piercing, ancient eyes at his guest—his rival for the souls of his people. This Pope's god, he knew, made the Incan obsession with sacred *huacas* pale by comparison. Saints, shrines, holy water... . He had studied it all, found it all incredible. There was only the Incan way. It had finally been proven.

Huascar sipped his coffee, joining his guest.

"I have spoken at length with Bartolomé de las Salas, your president," said Alejandro.

"You mean Peru's president." Huascar spoke in a low voice that came from deep within him. "The New Inca Church, of which I am head, does not know political boundaries. It is a vision, a way of life, the spirit of a people with a special destiny."

Pope Alejandro was silent a moment, then shrugged. He did not wish to be drawn in to this area. "Nevertheless, I have great respect for de las Salas, both as a man and as a leader. I have known him for more than thirty years—back to the time when he was a young lawyer who helped with church holdings in Lima and Caracas. A bright, insightful man. And an honorable one."

Huascar nodded.

"He says you can do it." The two men stared at each other in silence.

"I can," said Huascar. "Our time has come."

Alejandro chose his words carefully. "I approach you with an open mind."

Huascar smiled. The twinkle in his eyes was the pleasure of righteousness, of fulfillment achieved at long last. To have the Pope here, coming to him, afforded him a satisfaction that was profound. Eventually, he knew, they would all come to him. They would all be under his wing. The New Incas would rise triumphant, the instrument of the gods in shaping man's lot.

Huascar could not help the small vanity that allowed him to enjoy this. It was too exquisite to ignore.

None of it bothered Alejandro the way Huascar thought it might. The face of the Catholic pontiff betrayed nothing but a kind of philosophical largesse. Alejandro was the right man in the right place, Huascar thought. The gods know well what they do.

"If you approach us with an open mind, then it will happen."

"How does it happen? What makes it work?" Alejandro's questions were simple and to the point.

"It happens because it is time for it to happen. All things happen for this reason. It is like opening a door. It is like discovering that one's house contains many more rooms than one ever suspected. One goes from room to room, eventually arriving back at the point of departure, but with a new understanding of one's route through one's space and time."

"And the meteorite falls throughout South America?"

"Signs," said Huascar.

Alejandro waited.

"Signs from the sun god." He watched Alejandro carefully. The pontiff displayed none of the skeptical cynicism to which Huascar was inured. This is good, he thought. This man is everything that I have heard.

"The meteorites near Antofagasta, Chile, five years ago, started the power surging. The fall last year near Sao Paulo closed the circuit. The energy began to discharge. I am its medium." He shrugged, humbly. "You, surely, understand the concept of an earthly medium for a divine source. Was not your Jesus Christ such a medium? Do you not accept that he was capable of seemingly miraculous feats? Raising the dead? Water into wine? Surviving his own death?"

"Are you claiming divinity?"

Huascar watched the Pope's face carefully. There was no mockery there. It was an honest question.

"No," he said. "I am very human. I make no such claim."

"Why you, then?"

"Why Jesus? Why Mohammed? Why Gandhi? How can anyone know why one person becomes a catalyst for powerful historical and spiritual forces?" Again, he shrugged. "It merely is, that is all. I only know that this is something that I can do, something that I understand how to do. I don't know that I have been chosen. I only know that I have discovered the fact of my power. The 'why' of it will elude me, perhaps forever, or perhaps only until the picture becomes larger. I cannot see the whole picture yet. I may never see it, personally. It may be too vast."

"The meteorites lie along the Tropic of Capricorn. How is this important?"

"I do not know."

"Is their size significant?"

"I do not know."

Alejandro paused, thinking. "But you can do it?"

"I have done it. Several times."

Alejandro nodded. There had been many claims, but only the much-heralded testimony of de las Salas had brought the New Incas to the attention of the world media.

To travel back in time.

"De las Salas says that he visited his grandfather. He says that he spent a week with him in the year 1956."

Huascar nodded. "I believe this to be true. He disappeared, in front of more than four hundred people. Then, after seven days, he reappeared and told his story. I believe him. I believed the others. They *do* disappear.

They do come back. Where do they go? Why? It is always one hundred years in the past. Yet they do not consult with each other."

Pope Alejandro I stared hard at the Incan mystic.

Huascar gazed back at him, unwaveringly.

No one else said anything. The room was silent.

"I wish to try it," Alejandro said.

Huascar smiled. Then he nodded. "I would regard it as a great honor." He tilted his head respectfully. To send Alejandro back in time, he knew, would make him the new world religious leader. To succeed in this endeavor would assure the conversion of countless millions to the New Incas. It would signal the end of Catholicism as a force in South America —perhaps the world.

Alejandro was going to meet him head-on. If Huascar was a phony, then this would be the end of him. If he was truly capable of doing the thing he said he could, then Alejandro, too, knew what he was risking. To his credit, he placed truth above power and, with that ethic, there was no real risk.

If he can actually do this thing, Alejandro thought, then we should be following him.

"Who would you like to visit? An ancestor?"

"One of the great saints of our church. One of the truly selfless people of history."

Huascar waited without changing expression. He had cultivated patience to a fine art.

"Mother Teresa. Calcutta. One hundred years ago."

Even Huascar's inscrutable and weathered face brightened pleasantly at the challenge.

* * * * *

Three days later, the moon full, the communion meal taken, on the dais —the *usno*—in the center of Haucaypata Square, Pope Alejandro I, surrounded by four hundred New Incas and a sea of pageantry, shimmered, wavered, and disappeared from the sight of all.

Into the past.

Huascar smiled. The moment was his. Now, he thought.

They will all follow.

All.

3

NORFOLK ISLAND, SOUTH PACIFIC
BRITISH PENAL COLONY
2 February, 1835

"There's a new book in this month's shipment, Harriet. Something I shall look forward to reading." Major Joseph Anderson, Commandant of Norfolk Island, opened the volume on his lap and turned the pages with care. His wife continued with her work in the kitchen, offering only a polite "Oh?"

"A new angle on the *Bounty* disappearance. Looks fascinating."

Harriet Anderson had some difficulty drumming up the required enthusiasm for her husband's naval interests, but understood, neverthe-less, its importance for him. She knew, too, the pleasure such accounts afforded him—especially here, since his commission to Norfolk. Intellectual activity was something they both sorely missed. The books sent from London always helped.

"Didn't they send you a book on the *Bounty* already?"

"Yes. They did. Three months ago." He looked up and smiled a mock smile. "The so-called 'official' version: *The Eventful History of the Mutiny and Piratical Seizure of the Bounty.* It was published anonymously four years ago in London." He continued the mock smile. "It's public knowledge now, though, that it was written by Sir John Barrow, Secretary of the Admiralty—not exactly an objective account. Interesting, though. Tends to totally exonerate Bligh and condemn Fletcher Christian. Only natural, I guess, given the authorship."

"What's this one?"

Without his spectacles, he held the book at arm's length to read the title exactly. "*Narrative of a Voyage to the Pacific and Bering Strait.* Written by a Captain F W. Beechey." He flipped to the title page. "Published in London, 1831." He riffled a few more pages, pausing here and there. "Seems this Beechey fellow called in at Pitcairn in 1825 aboard the H.M.S. *Blossom,* and actually had an opportunity to peruse the fragmentary diary that Midshipman Young kept on the island." He glanced up at Harriet. "Sounds delightfully intriguing." His smile now was genuine.

"You don't like Bligh, do you?"

"It's not that at all." He seemed offended. "He was, by all accounts, a master seaman. It's not a case of liking or disliking him. It's a case of trying to understand how he must have erred in his judgement regarding the exercise of his authority. The line between firm discipline and respect and its obverse side, mutiny and rebellion, is a fine one. Bligh miscalculated, in the most infamous way. How? Why?"

He paused, musing. The questions were not idle to the commandant of Britain's most notorious penal colony.

Harriet entered the parlor from the kitchen, wiping her hands on a towel. She smiled at him benignly.

She was still a fine figure of a woman, he thought. There was gray in her hair after nineteen years of marriage and two children and innumerable assignments to the far-flung reaches of the globe with her husband. But she had borne her lot graciously, and his daughters did not seem the worse for their exotic travels and esoteric education. For all of this he loved her. And his daughters.

But the navy and his work were his first passion. His loyalty was to them. They had given him everything that he had wanted in life. He would not fail queen and country. He had learned much operating the prison in Van Diemen's Land, and what he had learned he wanted to apply here, on Norfolk.

He would study Bligh, find his error.

He would not fail.

*   *   *   *   *

At ten o'clock that morning, Major Anderson stood among four guards outside a low row of cells covered with a roof of mossy shingles. The turnkey opened the door. A yellow exhalation emerged, the produce of the bodies caged therein. Waiting until it dissipated, Anderson entered the room, flanked by the guards. Five men were chained to a traversing bar.

They were waiting to find out if they would live or die.

The stench of the cell was overwhelming, and Anderson fought back a wave of nausea as he stood there. Stepping aside, he let one of the guards pass and unlock the loose chain that held them to the wall. The three other guards, rifles poised, stayed as close to the door and the fresh air as they could.

Shackled now only by leg chains, the five men were led outside and into the center of the compound, where the ritual announcement could be made public. The prisoners who were not the objects of this particular sentence arrayed themselves at a prudent distance, yet close enough to view the spectacle and hear the pronouncements.

Anderson set his feet firmly and took a sheet of paper from his pocket. The prisoners stared at him with vacant eyes, unmoving.

"In the matter of the attempted escape from Norfolk Island and the attendant slaying of guard Peter Greenside, the council in Sydney, having heard and weighed the evidence, has reached the following verdicts. John Parker, Harry Douglas, and Malcolm Cooper—you are hereby sentenced to death by hanging, five days from now, on February 7, 1835. Robin Budd and Edward Grimble, you are hereby sentenced to serve an additional ten years each, here on Norfolk Island, upon the expiration of your initial sentences."

From an isolated corner of the compound, Bran Michael Dalton, the Irishman who was relatively new to Norfolk, watched the procedure. Every day brought him new and stunning information about this hellhole. But what he saw now topped them all.

He watched, shocked, as the three men who had just been sentenced to death fell to their knees, and with dry eyes, thanked God.

The two who had just heard their reprieve from the scaffold and their sentence of another ten years on Norfolk, slumped to the ground and wept bitterly.

Dalton began to understand the horrors of his new environment. And even though he was a grown man, he wished his Da was here with him now, to help him, to protect him, to comfort him, as he always had done.

But he was alone. There was not going to be any help.

It was taking a long time, but he was beginning to understand that.

4

SOUTH PACIFIC

1 June, 1972

"We're there, David."

McTaggart lifted his head from the charts he had been studying and stared at Grant, who was standing in the cabin entranceway. The swell that rocked them was gentle in comparison to the gales that had detained them for eight days in Rarotonga.

"The one-hundred-mile limit," he commented wryly.

Grant nodded.

"In defiance of all international law, they demand and expect an established 'off-limits' area of one hundred thousand square miles." He shook his head, grimacing. Then he glanced back at Grant, who was still waiting with a sense of anticipation for some sort of ceremonial signal of their penetration into the French cordon.

His face broke into a smile that he only half felt. "How does it feel to be entering the eye of the hurricane?"

"I think," said Grant, "that your metaphor is conservative." From behind his back he produced the bottle of champagne they had been saving. "Nigel and the others will be here shortly. Care for a drink?"

McTaggart smiled. "Yes. I think the occasion calls for it." He stood and went to get glasses from the cupboard. Standing with his back to Grant, his mind roamed freely for a few seconds, conjuring up the Mururoa Atoll out there in the night, some one hundred miles distant, the Uranium 235 mass an obscene blot on its tropical green and white lushness.

"Think we've been spotted yet?" he asked.

Grant shrugged. "Don't know. I guess so. They know we're coming. And they'll be patrolling the limits as a matter of form. No sign of them yet, though."

"Mm."

"What do you think they'll do? I mean, really?"

They had discussed the issue ad nauseam before leaving Auckland, but it had not been spoken of since. Only now did it seem real, now that they were here.

McTaggart eyed the Australian with affection, wondering what he had gotten this young man into. Then he remembered himself at the same age and smiled inwardly, knowing that no one got anyone into anything at that age—a twenty-six-year-old was completely capable of getting himself into everything. And then he thought of Ann-Marie, the lover he had left behind in Auckland, and felt a further sense of helplessness and loss sweep over him momentarily. He realized that only someone as wild and previously uncommitted as himself would get so completely and so spontaneously involved. Nevertheless, he now understood the arrogance and myopia of the French position—understood it more clearly as each day passed. He knew how the French had been testing atomic weapons for the past seven years over Mururoa, consciously ignoring the Atmospheric Test Ban Treaty signed by the U.S.A., Russia, and Great Britain in 1963. And he felt something akin to kismet summoning him, and searched constantly for its source without ever finding it.

Its source was out there.

Out there with the shoals and reefs, storms and high seas, military bases and guns, corvettes and helium balloons, and minesweepers and warships.

Out there.

"They can't explode the thing as long as we're around." Grant derailed his reverie.

They looked at each other in silence.

"Can they?"

McTaggart smiled whimsically, a faraway look in his eyes, his fingers tracing the new white that had been settling the past year in his sideburns.

II

Yes, as every one knows, meditation and water are wedded for ever.

Queequeg was a native of Kokovoko, an island far away to the West and South. It is not down in any map; true places never are.

Methinks we have hugely mistaken this matter of Life and Death.

— excerpts from Herman Melville's *Moby Dick*

II

* * 5 * *

LIMA, PERU
14 June, 2072

Fletcher Christian IV, along with his wife, Liana, was not surprised at the throng of reporters that descended upon them at the international airport. Their arrival, after all, was well-anticipated, and their intentions had made both eagerly-devoured soft and hard copy from Paris to Los Angeles to Cape Horn. Add to this the photogenic faultlessness of Liana's dusky Eurasian symmetry, and the only question that remained was merely the size of the media horde, not its appearance.

Nevertheless, it upset him. And his feelings, he knew, were as irrational in many ways as were his motives for coming. He could evince, both to himself and to others, rational, scientific inquiry as the primal pulse, and make it credible. But everyone, himself included, knew that there was more to it. He was, after all, Fletcher Christian IV, not John Doe, and his name glittered in the media with the aura of romance that his ancient forebear had bequeathed as his legacy for the last three hundred years.

Liana met his eyes, and he gripped her hand.

Flashes popped. The quartz lights for video and holo glared madly.

"Mr. Christian!" A voice rang out above the bustle. Airport security had created a V-shaped wedge for them to slide through to the waiting helicopter. "Are you really going to try to get back at Bligh? Or do you just want to sail on the *Bounty* for yourself?"

Christian stopped. Liana looked up at the lean, dark face that hinted at his heritage, worried that any crank utterance could disturb him. The surrounding horde quieted, waiting for his response.

His eyes searched the crowd. All the faces were the same, the source of the questions drowned in the potpourri of reporters. It's the heat, he thought. "At the gallery interview," he shouted back with the poise and control that had gotten him this far. "I'll deal with all questions there." And like visiting royalty, he even managed a smile and a brief wave, picking up stride once again with his wife, gripping her hand just a little too tightly for comfort.

The Atahualpa Gallery in central Lima had been chosen as the site of the televised interview for several reasons—reasons aesthetic, historical, and last but not least, theatrical.

Christian wandered about the spacious room, admiring the tastefully arrayed *objets d'art* that bespoke the heritage that was being reborn everywhere the Incas had held dominion: Ecuador, Peru, Chile, and much of Bolivia and Argentina. It was this very renaissance that was the manifestation of what had brought him here, to this land of humid mystery, to confront the ancient Huascar, and to see for himself.

Remarkably preserved ornate cooking vessels, bone flutes, wooden dolls, clay figurines from centuries ago—these were all displayed alongside more modern variations on similar themes: silver and gold wrought llamas, no taller than ten centimeters; reproduction textiles with Incan art, as had been found in mummy bundles; lacquered wooden beakers, intricate reproductions from the colonial period. He was entranced before a two-meter-square cloth panel unit that displayed—in the bright yet muted tones of the period of The Thirteen Emperors, some seven centuries ago—elaborate detail from a *queru,* the dance with the golden chain, when he heard his name.

Before turning to see who had summoned him so deferentially, he felt the hand on his elbow, comforting and friendly. It was the speaker— Alfred de Baudin, the expatriate Frenchman. He would be interviewing him, with unmatched linguistic fluency, in Christian's native English.

He smiled at the shorter man, who indicated with a tilt of his graying head the twin seats centered before the cameras. They were on.

Christian felt nervous, and was surprised. There was no reason for his anxiety: he was and always had been used to the media, and his own public-speaking itinerary was always full. The same apprehension had struck him upon landing at the airport, and he could only account for it by the magnitude of the expectations for his visit here. And the media seemed to sense it.

With a fully professional mien, de Baudin began. The event was live video—no taping—a rarity. Reporters, journalists, and other interpolators and intercessors for the world vidnetwork were hovering in the wings, shadows that would illuminate his mission for the vicarious pleasure of all.

"Fletcher Christian IV has graciously consented to discuss with us the momentous occasion of his visit to our fair land today." De Baudin turned toward Christian. "And we welcome you to Peru, Fletcher." He extended his hand in a demure ceremonial gesture.

Christian accepted the hand, shaking it firmly. "The pleasure's mine, Alfred."

"You're here to see Huascar." He was wasting no time.

Christian smiled. "I am."

"I think most of us know why—or, at least, some of the reasons. Perhaps the viewers might enjoy a little background on yourself—background that led up to the reasons for your visit here."

"Lots of things led me here. Which would you like to discuss?"

"You are, by profession, a scientist. Would you tell us about that?"

"Certainly." He shifted in the chair, adjusted his microphone. "I'm currently on sabbatical from my position as professor of Life Sciences at the University of Toronto. Before I became associated with the university, I was a project leader with the U.S.-Canada National Space-Time Administration Research Team. Last year I divided most of my time between teaching science history at the university and being science adviser to the president of Brazil. And I'm also president of the International Society for the Study of the Origin of Life."

"This is quite a litany of impressive posts, Fletcher, for a man so young."

"I wish I was as young as you apparently think I am." He smiled. "Sometimes I feel a lot older than my birth certificate indicates," he added, chuckling quietly. Out of the corner of his eye, off in the blurred recesses anterior to the glare of the video lights, he spotted Liana, and she smiled warmly, raising a hand; suddenly he didn't feel old at all. She had that effect on him.

"Tell us a bit more about the last post you cited—the one about the origin of life. I find it fascinating, and I'm sure viewers and listeners will too."

"It's quite an old and venerable society. The International Society for the Study of the Origin of Life held its first meeting over a century ago, in Moscow. It was 1957. The thirty-sixth conference was held two years ago, in Canberra. I'm currently preparing for the thirty-seventh conference, to be held next year, July 2073, in Kampala. The first few meetings of the society were sporadic, but for the past century we've held them like clockwork every three years."

"And all this is somehow tied in with your visit to Peru?"

"Oh, yes. Very much so." He paused. "Huascar and what appears to be his legitimate temporal transmissions are justifiably exciting. It's ironic, of course, that a society as firmly planted in science as ours, should eventually turn to methodology that is usually held askance by strict adherents to the 'scientific method'—of which I have always considered myself one. In defense, I can only say that the real superstition consists of rejecting things unexamined. There appears to be enough evidence to conclude that something very real is in fact occurring at Cuzco, under the auspices of Huascar. By the way," he added, "Huascar makes me feel young."

De Baudin smiled. "He's eighty-seven, according to what I can recall. And Fletcher, how old are you, for the record?"

"I'm forty-six."

"And your lovely wife?"

"Let's just say that youth still shines kindly and brightly on her, Alfred, and that I am the beneficiary of the glow that reflects from her."

"Spoken like a poet."

"I'm a great admirer of poetic truth. Quite often the truth is clearer on an intuitive level than it can ever be on a scientific level." His eyes met Liana's, infusing his blood with the reality of his words. She smiled back, a smile only for him.

"Your visit here, then, could be seen as a radical departure from your previous courses of investigation, as well as the courses followed over the years by other members of the society."

"I like to think that it is a logical course of investigation, illustrating our open-mindedness, rather than a radical departure in procedure, as you suggest. I do, however, see the graceful irony in eventually approaching a man like Huascar, who has made his reputation as a mystic over the years. But the facts remain: he seems to have opened a gate of some kind, and it may well herald the onset of a new era of necessary fusion between the hard sciences and what I can only call, imprecisely, the powers of the mind. More accurately, though, I suspect that most, if not all, of whatever Huascar is achieving can ultimately be explained scientifically. But until then, we are quite willing to merely utilize the facts as they appear, sifting them into component parts as we can."

"You're suggesting that Huascar's contention—the contention of the

New Inca Church, in fact—that the meteorite falls of the past twenty years in Brazil and Chile are signs from the sun god that something momentous is about to occur, might be less than accurate." De Baudin smiled knowingly.

"It's an interesting poetic interpretation. But it's not even necessary to believe that, to see that something is happening. The strange, and probably purely coincidental, alignment of the meteorites along the Tropic of Capricorn, combined with some truly phenomenal psychic power that Huascar is either privy to or host for, has all colluded to drop into our collective lap the opportunity of a lifetime. And I think it's all pointing at me, strangely enough, both because of my heritage and because of my position as president of the society."

"What possible scientific explanation could you offer that might help our viewers understand that there might be a completely traceable cause and effect for all this?"

"I don't really have such an explanation to offer your viewers, Alfred. I can mention a few areas that are wide open to further investigation, though."

"Please do. This is fascinating."

"Well, it's been established that meteorites are much more than lifeless hunks of rock. The simplest life forms, known to most people as viruses, are merely DNA molecules with a bit of protein coating them. DNA molecules are made of nucleic acids, which in turn are made of compounds called bases. And proteins are made from amino acids. Years ago, amino acids were found in fragments of meteorites, and shortly after that discovery, bases were found in the fragments as well. Simply put, meteorites have in them what we could call the elements of life, and meteors have been showering the planet from its earliest days."

"Are you saying that this could be the origin of life?"

Christian shrugged. "It's a possibility."

"And that this could somehow be tied in with Huascar's temporal projection capability?"

"Again, it's possible. There's too much that we just don't know yet. I could be way off base. But the point I wanted to make was that the notion of a meteorite from the sun god might be merely a poetic expression of a more serious scientific reality, which, if combined with other scientific realities, could present us with brand-new data, brand-new areas of investigation. And, in this case, it's particularly exciting because we might—just might—get a chance to get a retrospective look at our history. Granted, the range of the experience as it now seems to exist, is one hundred years; but if we can harness the methodology, understand it, then perhaps we can learn to use it, the way we learned to use our discovery of electricity, or our discovery of solar energy, or of nuclear power. And I do think that this discovery could be as big, if not bigger, than the last three I just mentioned."

"You think, then, that Huascar is capable of temporal transmission of a willing and suitable subject?"

"Within certain limitations, that seems to have been already established. One of your own presidents, the late de las Salas, was the first public figure to provide credible testimony to that effect. Pope Alejandro I's detailed visitation with Mother Teresa back in 1956 was equally heralded. Since then, there've been more than a dozen equally credible testimonials, all amply supported by verifiable minutiae. And now, beyond the potential personal and historical research posited by such a discovery, the Society for the Study of the Origin of Life can see that this is the obvious area of pursuit for our own research. The key would seem to be the ability to understand and control the process more extensively, in order to expand the range of the transmissions beyond a century or so. If we could ever manage to drop the limiting temporal range, then the door is cast wide on mankind's ability to finally know the truth about his origins. This, we feel, is the most exciting possibility in the history of pure scientific investigation."

Christian's enthusiasm was beginning to emerge, and the audience sensed that it was genuine, as did de Baudin. The interviewer pursued this fervor. "We understand some of your concern to study—even to try—Huascar's power, as the president of your society, even as a scientist in general. Could you talk to us a bit about your own personal heritage and its, shall we say, 'advantage,' in this undeniably strange and fascinating matter?"

Fletcher smiled and looked down at his hands, folded in his lap. "I'd think," he said, "that video patrons, and whatever film-going public remains, would have had a surfeit of information—both true and mythical—about my illustrious forebear." He paused, aware that this topic was always inevitable, and tugged deep inside himself for the necessary resolve to delineate some of the highlights once more, in what seemed to be an interminable chant of mostly stale detail. With renewed good will, he persevered. He looked up at de Baudin. "I am the direct descendant of *the* Fletcher Christian, the famous—or infamous—master's mate who marshaled the mutiny of her majesty's ship *Bounty,* on April 28, 1789, near Tofua, in the seductive blue waters of the South Pacific." The wry tone, barely perceptible, nevertheless elicited an understanding smile from de Baudin. Fletcher Christian IV continued. "Huascar's most successful temporal transmissions all involved subjects with very powerful historic personalities, along a highly defined set of latitudinal parameters. In most cases, this entailed a projection along the path somehow preordained by the meteorite falls—namely along the Tropic of Capricorn. Huascar himself is on record as saying that it is a tribute to the strength and historic auras of both Pope Alejandro I and Mother Teresa that he was able to transcend this usual limitation and make the spatial leap to the latitude of the Tropic of Cancer, where it passes through India, near Calcutta."

"Why do you think these Tropic zones figure so prominently in the transmissions?"

"We simply don't know yet. They represent the boundaries of the equatorial zone, the planet's warmest tract. This, apparently, has great bearing on Huascar's ability. The reasons, at this point, are purely speculative."

"This ties in neatly with the New Inca's belief in the sun god, and its power on earth."

Christian shrugged. "It does."

"But you don't give the notion much credence."

"The sun seems to have an effect. What more can I say?"

"And how does it figure in your own quest?"

"If you study a map of the world, or even of a prescribed area of the South Pacific from South America to Australia, you'll see that the Tropic of Capricorn passes through many of the places associated with my own ancestors. Well, not literally through such places but close enough to polarize whatever temporal transmissions might pierce the area. It pervades Pitcairn Island, where the *Bounty* mutineers eventually settled; it passes within range of Tahiti, where the episode began and whence Fletcher Christian took his wife, Mi'Mitti; and it is not overly far from Norfolk Island, which Britain offered to the Pitcairners for resettlement after it had been abandoned as a penal colony in 1855. In short, it seems to penetrate my ancestral past with uncanny precision. Given my position as president of the society, my unique ancestry, and the coincidence of the Capricorn Connection, it seems to be a form of inescapable kismet, all channeled toward me." He paused. "It is, you must admit, rather exciting."

"For onlookers as well, Fletcher, I assure you."

"Yes. I guess so." He looked back down at his folded hands.

"Is it true that Huascar is still the only one of his circle who can effect the transmissions?"

"It would appear so."

"He's eighty-seven. What happens when he's gone?"

"This is one of the reasons why we must strive to understand the process as soon as possible. It is one of the reasons why I am here now. If we do not use our time efficiently, we may never apprehend Time at all."

* * 6 * *

NORFOLK ISLAND
6 March, 1835

Bran Michael Dalton gazed at the slop spooned from the dank, black pot, and had to force himself, as he did daily, not to retch. With the effort came the familiar physical shudder throughout his body, a shudder that signaled, to him, a further weakening, a continuation of the slide of his muscles and flesh into the inevitable decrepitude of the other prisoners about him.

Shuffling listlessly to the end of the closest wooden bench, he sat and contemplated his meal. The potatoes were the only recognizable things in the colorless gruel-like paste on his plate; the aroma that emanated from it reminded him of the conglomeration of inedible scraps that was left behind in bowls under the table for the dogs back in Dublin, the city that once had seemed unbearable, but which now glistened in his memory with more saving graces than he could ever have imagined previously.

He glanced at the fellow beside him. "What is this?"

The scraggy, sallow mate examined the portion on his own plate with a jaundiced eye. Then he turned a gaunt face and one watery blue eye—the other closed with an enormous sty—toward Dalton. "English puke, I believe. Mixed with rat meat and some of your own dear Irish spuds."

He then bent his face toward the plate and began to tilt some of the substance toward his mouth.

"This stuff needs a spoon," Dalton muttered.

A guard who had picked up the half-volume mutter turned and stared at him, with something very akin to relish. A second passed, then another, as Dalton realized he had been heard, and waited to see if it would be ignored or followed up. Apparently, this was not his lucky day.

The guard stalked over toward him slowly. He was brutish and balding, with a face that hinted at little intelligence. "Did you have somethin' you wanted to say?" He waited, a cat with a mouse.

Dalton knew better. Everyone on the island knew better. But sometimes knowing better can't stop the urge to state the obvious, to tell the truth, to demand, however meekly, some small measure of reason, of justice. So he stared up at the man, with whatever tiny vestige of dignity and defiance that had not yet taken flight from the environment that smothered him. The fellow beside him froze, motionless, as did others within hearing distance. For this reason too, Dalton felt challenged, and was aware that his humiliation might be worse if he backed down under the scrutiny of his mates.

He could not win.

Nor could he remain silent.

"This stuff," he repeated, gazing boldly at his gaoler, "needs a spoon."

A smile of delight spread across the guard's face. He could scarcely believe the opportunity. Before Dalton could blink, the butt of the guard's rifle struck him viciously along the cheekbone and temple, splitting the skin and knocking Dalton off the end of the bench. He slumped down on the floor against the wall, a great crimson flow oozing from the rent on his face, spreading along his neck and under his collar.

Nobody in the room moved or spoke for several seconds. Then, gradually, it became obvious that the challenger had been quelled, and that the event, for the main part, had concluded.

Normal rhythms of motion resumed. The sty-eyed man bent himself once more to his self-serving task, inured as he was for years now about the lack of eating utensils.

Two other guards approached. "Problem?"

The one who had struck Dalton looked up at the one who had just spoken. "He wanted a spoon." The smile that followed spread slowly over his face, prompting similar displays of incredulity mixed with pleasure from the other two. They all turned to stare at Bran Michael Dalton, the recently arrived prisoner from the slums of Dublin, who, so dearly needed to be taught the tacit rules of behavior on the island—rules that they were more than willing to impart.

The two new guards bent and dragged Dalton to his feet, conscious of avoiding the spillage of blood onto their own clothing.

Nobody dared look up as Dalton was escorted from the room, alternately walking of his own accord and being held upright between the duo of turnkey escorts.

*   *   *   *   *

Norfolk Island: *largest of a group of islands situated 930 miles east-northeast of Sydney, latitude 29°3' South and longitude 167°56' East; the group consists of Norfolk and Philip Islands, some six miles apart, along with others, including Nepean and Bird Islands, which consist of little more than barren rocks surrounding the main island. Norfolk is not quite five miles in length, with a median width of approximately two and one-half miles. The group was a discovery of Captain Cook on 10 October 1774. Its coastline is inhospitable, without a harbour, washed by heavy surf and thus difficult of access except in favourable weather. It is, after Sydney, the oldest English settlement in the Pacific.*

— Encyclopedia Australiana,
Vid hardcopy ex., cr. ref., 15 June 2072

*   *   *   *   *

Bran Michael Dalton, twenty-nine years of age, had spent most of his youth and adulthood performing the honest and honorable task of delivering coal to the manors of the Anglo-Irish in and around Dublin. This had not stopped him from engaging in many of the less than honest and less than honorable pastimes that occupied most of his peers in the Catholic slums; nevertheless, he was one of a kind in many ways—always capable and ready to perform a day's honest toil for whatever the going rate was—which was always far less than honest in the sway of balance held by his English employers. But the balance of trade scarcely concerned him. It was out of his hands. He left the question of rights to those with more bullheadedness than he himself would admit to—an irony upon which he had dwelt at length these last several months.

It had been an incident with his less than veridical and conscionable peers that had brought him so far from home, in a way that he could never have imagined in his most feverish nightmares, to this forsaken penitence. He recalled the melee with the English sailors on the quays, the whisky, the subsequent and—even as it was happening—regrettable break-in at the warehouse and the unfocused sacking of the tea chests that were all they found there. He remembered grimly, too, how it had been only he who had been apprehended, how his mates had all managed to escape through the window on the second floor, how he had been alone on the main floor when the door burst open.

Uneducated and untutored, he had stood before the magistrate alone, and listened with only an inkling of the import of the judgement against him as he was sentenced to seven years' transportation.

And there seemed to be no end to his self-destruction, he thought, as he once more found himself standing alone, defenseless, before the island's commandant, Major Joseph Anderson.

His hands were shackled; his face caked with the blood that still oozed redly along his jawline and down his neck. But buried deep within him, as yet unassailable, lay the intractable spirit which had gotten him this far. His Da, he knew, would be proud. There was only so much an Irishman could take from these English fuckers. He had heard it often, believed it with a passion, and expressed it with zeal when the moment arrived, as it did on occasion.

After only a month on the island, he had been the recipient of one hundred lashes and forced to wear irons for a week. Walking back along the narrow path from the latrine, he and two other prisoners had been confronted by an officer. His two mates knew the routine, and even though it meant standing in six inches of rainwater in the ditch at the path's side, they stepped aside. Dalton had refused to remove himself so humbly, trying to force a squeezed pass.

He had paid the price.

It seemed he would always pay the price, and the glint of pride and defiance had not yet dimmed from his fierce eyes.

He stared hard and straight at Anderson. In return, the commandant regarded him with a mixture of curiosity and disdain.

It was the commandant who broke the silence. "I understand, Mr. Dalton, that you have caused trouble this evening at dinner." His voice was laced with a practiced ennui, the edge of which remained cuttingly sarcastic.

Dalton did not respond.

Allowing the proper few seconds to elapse, Anderson continued to amass his case. "And," he paused, sighing dramatically, "you've been to see me before." He scratched the side of his neck, appearing momentarily distracted. This done, he once again stared hard at Dalton. "Is there anything you'd like to say that might influence my decision of the next few minutes?"

Dalton stared back at Anderson unflinchingly. This seemed to partially amuse the commandant, judging from the twinkle that began to shimmer in the man's eyes.

Yes, Dalton thought. I'm sure I could say many things that might influence your decision. I could beg for mercy. I could drop to my knees. I could apologize to that shite who would never have had the balls to hit me anywhere but here, on this island, where he's sure there can never be any calling to account.

He continued to stare at the major, whose reputation was that of an emasculated fop among both prisoners and guards alike. "I did," he said, finally, "nothing to merit this." It was all he wanted to say. It was the truth, unadorned, without passion.

In response, Anderson's face flushed, and he rose to his feet from behind the massive desk. He pointed a snaky finger at his prisoner. His breathing was labored, and he was on the brink of rage. "You are here," he said, through clenched teeth, "both on this island and in this room, because you have done everything to deserve being here." He leaned forward, his eyes forced to look up in deference to Dalton's superior height. "Is that understood?"

The last word was punctuated with a sharp jab of his finger in Dalton's direction. The finger, Dalton noted, curled very slowly and shakily back into the commandant's closed fist.

Dalton could feel the warmth of his own blood trickling down his face. He blinked away the sweat from his eyes and continued to stare in silence. Finally, he shrugged, a sense of resignation tempered with what, in more favorable circumstances, could have been termed indifference settling like a Dublin fog throughout his body. He was ready to take whatever outrage they bestowed upon him. He had done it before. He could do it again.

The commandant seemed to understand this acceptance, and found it a taunt to his authority. How, he wondered, can I instil fear in these animals if they don't learn that the consequences for any type of insubordination are intolerable?

And this Dalton… He was among the worst. It was almost impossible to scare or hurt him.

The commandant's eyebrows furrowed as Dalton waited. He knew what he had to do with this prisoner.

He had to make an example of him. Once and for all.

✳ ✳ 7 ✳ ✳

LIMA, PERU

14 June, 2072

Liana Christian was, in fact, thirty-two years old. Her father had been English, her mother Malaysian, and the resultant hybrid seated with her long legs crossed on the hotel room's settee, bore lush testimony to the richness of both lines.

Entering the room from the tiny kitchenette, a scotch and water in each hand, Fletcher paused. No matter how often he feasted his eyes on her, he never ceased to be amazed at her beauty.

He never ceased to be amazed the she was his.

She caught him looking, and smiled a knowing, encouraging smile. Although they had been married only a year, their three years of cohabitation had made them intimately aware of the subtle nuances in each other's behavior. The gallery interview had left Fletcher tense and fatigued, and Liana wanted him to relax. He needed to relax.

Lifting one foot to the top of the coffee table in front of her, she let her silk robe fall open along the lines of her legs.

His eyebrows rose up above the rims of his classic spectacles. A smile teased at the corner of his mouth.

He crossed the room, placing the glasses on the table—one on each side of her foot. Her toes curled tightly, then relaxed gradually.

When he sat down beside her, she took his hand and placed it on her thigh, then reached over and began to systematically undo the buttons on the front of his shirt.

He remembered their first night together, at her apartment in Singapore, almost five years ago. It brought back a collage of images and memories: a heady mixture of French scents and Asian light; the wicker furniture and bamboo curtains, long shadows from the oil lamp. After what seemed like an eternity in academe, Liana's induction to the world of sensuality had scalded him. Fletcher Christian IV, renowned among his peers and the world scientific community, had not known that a woman like her existed. It had seemed to be the stuff of fiction, based on his strictly defined experience. I had seemed a dream.

Yet she was real.

*   *   *   *   *

His senses drowned in Singapore, Kuantan, wind-chimes, and warm breezes, as she opened to him.

"We haven't touched our drinks." She moved her hand.

He inhaled sharply at her touch. "They won't go bad. They never do."

Like a drug, the pleasure consumed him. He pressed her backward onto the settee.

"Wait."

He blinked, listening above the pounding of his own heart. Her dark green eyes flashed around the room. "There," she said.

His eyes followed her gaze.

"There," she repeated.

His eyebrows raised appreciatively, his mouth parting in wonder. And he smiled the smile of a man too fortunate to tamper with such an offer. "How fitting," he said. "And how interesting."

"Every good scientist knows that an experiment should seek to be interesting." She paused. "As well as fruitful."

They both stared at the large desk on the far side of the room.

And Fletcher also found it interesting how that evening of pleasure, in the hotel room in Lima, Peru in June 2072, was the evening that he always returned to in his memories of Liana. Her exciting offer, the world ahead of them, the wanton and perfect sensuality of their union, the city spread out below them like a hothouse jewel, glimmering and winking in the humid night—it all coalesced to cap their arrival in the land of the New Incas unforgettably.

For how could he have known that it would be one of their last times together? If he had known, could he possibly have savored it more?

He knew that he could not. Hindsight enshrined it, as it did most things.

$* \quad * \quad 8 \quad * \quad *$

MURUROA ATOLL

16 June, 1972

"Where's Nigel?" McTaggart turned to see Grant coming up out of the cabin.

"Sleeping."

"Sleeping?"

"Well, lying down, anyway. Says he's got a bit of a bug of some kind. I think he's just naturally depressed." Grant smiled. "You know—back to the womb, all that stuff. Foetal position."

McTaggart smiled wryly. He seemed to be only half listening.

"What are you thinking about?"

McTaggart turned toward him. "What else?"

"Yeah. I know." He placed his hands on the rail alongside McTaggart. They both stared out across the morning swells.

"You know," McTaggart began, "the average tourist to Tahiti hasn't got a clue."

Grant frowned.

"To them, it's utopia. Gauguin's paintings. Bare-breasted lovelies smiling while they dance." He paused. "There are two thousand French military personnel and five hundred French civilians working on the bomb—most of them living on Mururoa Atoll, three hours by DC6 from their four-star hotels. The British and the Americans monitor the whole works from the sea and air. Even the Russians show up irregularly, wanting everybody to believe that they really are fishing trawlers—slightly off-course." He shook his head.

Grant said nothing.

"And the UN is holding an environmental conference in Stockholm this week. You can bet that the misuse of nuclear energy will be put in a cupboard and forgotten." His voice was matter-of-fact.

He looked at Grant. "Do we really have a chance?"

Grant put his hand to his forehead.

"I mean," McTaggart continued, "in the face of such monumental indifference, does anybody really even care?"

Grant didn't know what to say. It had all been said.

"Look at this." McTaggart took a piece of paper from his jacket pocket. The wind bent the corner over onto his hand. He pressed it back.

"This is what's out there against us." He held the paper out to Grant.

"What is it?"

"Look at it."

Grant took the paper, holding it against the wind in both hands.

"It's the specs on the French fleet."

Grant stared at it without speaking.

"See the size of those fucking things?"

Grant said nothing.

"Information from Auckland this morning. Lists of information. Stats. Data. Not too much in the way of conclusions. Guess they don't want to scare us. We're supposed to draw our own conclusions."

The wind whipped at the fragile paper. A gull screeched. "There's a command cruiser, the *De Grasse,* with a complement of 560, plus accommodation for 120 engineers and technicians. Three of the others—they're armed, by the way—are ex-Canadian ships. They were 'gifts' from Canada to France, to be restricted to NATO use."

"NATO?"

McTaggart nodded.

"What're they doing here then?"

McTaggart snorted. "I guess they're like the Russian trawlers. I guess they foundered slightly off-course."

"From the North Atlantic to the South Pacific. Why hasn't anyone said anything?"

"No one will listen. Besides, everybody is holding everybody else's hand."

"Business partners," Grant muttered.

"Yeah. Business."

Grant handed the paper back to McTaggart. He pocketed it in silence.

*   *   *   *   *

"It had been explained to me by the RAF monitor that the counter measured a safe level of radiation by clicking once every ten seconds. Well, two days after one of those tests, it rained, and the rain was drifting down from Mururoa. They had set the equipment up in a shed adjacent to my schoolhouse. I couldn't help but hear it. The thing was clicking like a damn rattlesnake. The RAF bloke came into my schoolhouse—right in the middle of class—quite shaken. Said that we should do something. I asked him 'What?' He didn't know."
— excerpt from an interview with a Pitcairn schoolteacher, recalling an incident in the early 1970s

*   *   *   *   *

McTaggart thought often about Ann-Marie. She should be here with me, he thought. I need her. This is unnatural, being without a woman for so long—especially the woman you want. I won't travel without her again, he vowed.

She was twenty years his junior. Gene's—his friend's—daughter. Yet Gene accepted it. So did everybody else. Ann-Marie was studying English at the University of Waikato and exhibited all the intelligence and sensitivity of the best of the educated youth of her generation. McTaggart had been infected by her sense of commitment to a cause. It had been Ann-Marie, he knew, who was responsible for him being here now, clutching this rail, rolling with the swell of the South Pacific beneath him. Challenge.

She had challenged him.

McTaggart had planned on sailing *Vega* to Australia, across the Indian Ocean, through the Atlantic to the Mediterranean. And he had planned on taking Ann-Marie with him.

An uninhibited pleasure cruise. Travel. Adventure. Aimless.

She had challenged him to do something significant after they had discussed the outrage of the French testing. He recalled his protests to her. A task for young people, he had asserted. She had dismissed his excuses. He was free. He had the time. He had the opportunity. He had the skill, the boat, the knowledge. He could come up with no reason *not* to do it.

He had the responsibility. Everyone did. She made him see that.

That was what the young could do that he could not do himself: hold up the mirror for him to see himself and his life more clearly.

Ann-Marie could do this for him. He loved her for it. She gave him his rebirth, in so many ways. It was something precious and fragile and wonderful, this chance to live with someone whose beauty shone through into her idealism, and in whose light his own jaded cynicism had been suffused.

He wanted her so badly that he ached.

*   *   *   *   *

"The French claim their possession of nuclear bombs and other weapons of mass destruction will greatly assist in maintaining liberty in the world, and that therefore it is essential for them to carry out the proposed tests... The people of Pitcairn are living in fear of what the future holds for their island. Why should we, a helpless handful of people, be swept aside like straws in the wind?"

> —editorial in the *Pitcairn Miscellany*, June 1963. (A monthly mimeographed sheet, written by the island schoolmaster, and Pitcairn's closest approximation to a newspaper.)

*   *   *   *   *

His belly full with dinner, McTaggart ascended to the cockpit to scan the horizon. The sun was sitting on the water in lush, red, tropical splendor, the breeze mild, and there was still no sign of other ships. Lifting his eyes to the sky, he shaded his brow with his hand and watched a lone, gray gull soaring high above. For several seconds he followed the bird's path, both admiring its graceful glide and identifying with its strange, self-imposed isolation. Seconds later the gull was gone, slipped into some optical crevice of light that struck McTaggart's eyes as he stared too directly at the sun. Blinking, he refocused, and saw something else.

It hovered in the clouds, due west, over the area that would be Mururoa. McTaggart squinted, straining his vision. Helicopter? he wondered. It still wasn't clear.

He descended back into the cabin to get the binoculars. Emerging from below, he raised them to his eyes and stared at the airborne object. The ketch bobbed, making his task take longer than he wanted. He searched.

Clouds. Water. Sun glinting off water.

There. There it was.

Jesus, he thought. It can't be.

He continued to stare, the adrenaline flushing through his body.

Slowly, he let the binoculars fall to his chest and hang there limply.

Grant emerged from the cabin below. "What is it?"

Turning, McTaggart stared at him. "It's a balloon," he heard himself saying. "It's a fucking great balloon."

Tugging the binoculars away from him, Grant looked for himself. Slowly, he too let them fall from his eyes. He turned to stare at McTaggart. "The bastards," he said. Then, as if thinking again, he looked once more, longer this time. Beneath the binoculars his mouth tightened grimly. "It's like the Frenchman told us: when they get ready to blow off the bomb, they lift it aloft with a balloon."

"And," McTaggart answered, "they said in Auckland that when you could see the balloon, you were too close. Said that you could forget everything else. That you couldn't get away in time." His face looked drawn and haggard, as if perhaps they had played too hard, perhaps misjudged, perhaps lost the highest stakes of all.

The balloon was still hanging there in the sky when night fell. But the darkness did not manage to erase it from their minds. Each of them could still see it clearly and starkly, especially if they closed their eyes, long after the sun had set.

It was almost midnight when McTaggart made the decision. "I think," he said, "that we should go closer."

The others stared at him.

"Maybe fifteen miles away."

Nobody replied.

"Force their hand."

At dawn, they moved out. The balloon was still there, about a thousand feet off the ground. The wind was blowing out of the west, across the atoll, directly toward them, reminding everyone on board of the dark, invisible seeds that it might sow at any minute.

"Suppose they actually do it," Nigel said.

They all looked at him.

"Set it off, I mean."

"It's a bluff," Grant said. For support, he looked to McTaggart.

McTaggart shrugged his shoulders, his face expressionless. "Suppose it's not," Nigel countered. He too looked toward McTaggart.

Sighing, McTaggart realized that they were waiting for him to deal with it, in some way they could understand. He was the leader. It was up to him.

He tilted his head and rubbed the side of his neck with what seemed to be thoughtless distraction, but which was really giving him more time to think, to evaluate. Sighing once more, he paused, then dug down deep for more conviction and assurance than he felt.

He stared at them unflinchingly. "Then let's get ready for it," he said.

They placed the wooden plugs beside each of the ketch's vents, ready to be hammered into place to seal the interior as tightly as possible. A straw vote would decide which of them would go on deck afterward, covered in oilskins, to attempt to sail the boat out of the danger zone. A hose was lowered from the craft's Honda generator pump to thirty feet below the water's surface—below where they calculated the fallout would reach—in order to have access to uncontaminated water in case they needed to douse flames on either the deck or in the sails.

All of this was, of course, assuming that they survived the initial blast.

That night, McTaggart had a dream. Even the next day, he could not shake it.

He dreamed that he was with Ann-Marie on the boat. His daughters were there too. In the dream, the sun turned hideous, a bright orange, expanding upward, elongating, its final shape the horrific emblem of devastation: the mushroom.

They sailed into the sun, into the mushroom, into the mad, tumescent orange flames.

And through them.

On the other side, his daughters had daughters, and they in turn had daughters, and Ann-Marie had aged, turning from a blonde beauty into graying matron. They were all on the boat together, sailing away from the madness at their backs. The heat of the flames seared his neck, burning the hairs off the nape.

But he was afraid to turn around.

He could not look back upon such naked power. So, surrounded by his progeny, he went ahead. There was no going back. Not ever.

But he could see nothing ahead, either.

Even the waking hours of daylight did little to ease the starkness of his nighttime reverie.

He clung, staring, to the rail, for most of the next day.

For days, the balloon hovered above them. And they waited under its brooding embrace, silent most of the time, feeling small and very alone.

Although not a religious man, McTaggart wondered if he should pray.

* * 9 * *

LIMA, PERU
16 June, 2072

Fletcher Christian IV punched off the televideo with an air of exasperation and pushed the castor chair back through the deep-pile carpet in the
hotel suite.

Liana eyed him warily. "What is it?"

Swiveling, he stared at her. "Two weeks," he said.

She frowned.

"It won't be for two weeks." He tilted his head and grimaced. Then,
slowly, he inhaled deeply, coming to some kind of terms with the news.
His eyebrows lifted, and he let a wry smile surface. "That was Huascar's
top aide, fellow chief-mystic, whatever. Said that Huascar would perform
the temporal transmission of yours truly back to Pitcairn Island in the
year of our Lord, 1972, on July 1st—not sooner. I reminded him that we
had an agreement to attempt the transmission on June 20. Didn't seem to
perturb him greatly that he was failing to live up to the timeline. I guess
you can do that—postpone at will—if you're the world's only known successful temporal transmitter, even if your subject has traveled halfway
around the world to participate." A half-laugh escaped him. "So," he continued, "we're off to Cuzco, yes, but not for at least another ten days as

I see it."

Liana approached him, placing her hands on his shoulders in comfort. At her touch, he relaxed; at her scent, the delay seemed to wane in priority.

"Lima is a pretty exciting place to spend ten days," she said. "You're just anxious."

It was true. He was anxious. And apprehensive. And impatient. In fact, he was literally counting the hours, and had been for weeks now.

"I'm not even sure I want you to go," she said, her eyes softening.

"I understand."

"It's like voodoo or something."

"This is the twenty-first century."

"That's what I mean. Mystics. Time travel. It's weird."

"And science. Don't forget the meteorites."

"But you don't even understand it."

He shrugged. "No. Not really."

"It might all be a sham."

"It's possible. I doubt it, though."

They continued to stare at each other.

"Anyway," he said, "we'll find out. Won't we?"

She smiled back at him. Then she bent and brushed her lips along the side of his neck. "Our dinner reservation isn't until eight." She inclined her head toward the wall-digital. "And it's only five-thirty."

He followed her glance to the stark blue digits. Then he turned his chair flush toward her, placed his hands on the crescents of her hips, and pressed his lips against the soft bowl of her belly.

10

NORFOLK ISLAND

7 March, 1835

Dalton could feel the maggots gorging on the wounds that streaked his back. They had nestled into the open purple and red gashes, and into the pulpy, white flesh that edged the sickly perimeter of the affected area. The hot climate nurtured them; it was up to the likes of him to feed them.

It was, he thought, lying on his side, another of the island's many features.

One hundred lashes. Again.

And this.

It was night. Without the roof of the barracks above him, he watched the stars, brilliant and fierce, remote and mysterious. They were allies. He understood their cold distance. Their silence was their armor. He was alone with them. There was nobody else. There never would be anyone else, he now began to see.

He tried shifting his weight, only to halt abruptly as a wave of pain engulfed him. If a rib wasn't broken, then it was so badly bruised that the difference was not significant.

Nor could he comfortably lie on his back for fear that he would infect the welts there more than they may already be infected. With no way to wash them, the scabs would form over the dirt from the ground on which he was lying, and Bran Michael Dalton didn't fully comprehend what the ultimate result could be. He wasn't sure if it could kill him or not. He was sure that he still cared, though. He still wanted to live. They hadn't managed to beat that out of him, as they had so many others he had seen.

He thought of his Da. His Da would be proud of him.

With his left hand, he found himself gripping with manic strength, just for a moment, the twenty-six foot chain that girded his waist, the far end of which was fastened to the boulder that would be the pivotal source of his radius for the next two weeks—two weeks during which no one else was allowed to talk to him, or even to acknowledge him.

He gripped the steel umbilical cord that refused to release him into the world. It had always been like this for him, he thought. The cord shrank or loosened, mutated in texture or form, but never disappeared. He believed for some, it did disappear; and he knew that for others, it never did.

The rain, later that night, soothed him. When sleep came, it was in the form of delirious exhaustion.

He dreamed that he and his Da were both chained to the rock, and that they were able to move it by pitting their strength against it one moonless night, rolling it toward the commandant's house, through it, and into the sea.

He dreamed that they hugged one another, the rain falling in torrents about them, washing away both blood and tears. But it was only a dream.

* * **11** * *

LIMA, PERU

23 June, 2072

"I don't understand," Liana said. "What's a *huaca?*"

"It's a kind of sacred object, in its simplest terms," Fletcher replied. "It might be the most significant concept in the deciphering of Incan culture."

"And Cuzco is a *huaca?*"

"The most significant one."

"I thought they were smaller things—objects with almost fetishistic importance. You told me one time that *huacas* included rocks, springs, caves, tombs, mummified bodies—things like that."

"They do. Even the meteorite fragments in Chile and Brazil qualify. The veneration of these items is like the relicolatry and iconolatry of Christianity. The Shroud of Turin. Lourdes. Like that."

"Is Cuzco like the Vatican then?"

Christian considered this. "Interesting parallel. Yes. In a way, I guess you could say that." He paused, then elaborated. "The Incas inhabited Cuzco not merely because of convenience or tradition, but because it was the only *huaca* that contained the plenitude of their past history, their present existence, and their perceived destiny. At one time there were over four hundred shrines in the city. The place was full of, for want of a better word, 'mystery.' The Incan people were their own priests, serving their greatest *huaca;* it's what the New Incas are reviving. They want no professional, or ordained intermediaries, placed between them and the holy environment. They are all, in their particular canon, in touch with the sacred. Few people have ever felt this as strongly."

They gazed out at the modern urban bustle of the street on which they were lunching. Their table was ecocontrolled by tabletop dials and sun-reducing dome. Liana was struck by the stark contrast with what they had just been discussing. She stirred her fork vaguely through her salad.

"Cuzco is definitely where it must occur," he added, finally.

"And you must be a part of it."

He looked up from his plate. "I want to be a part of it." Liana poked slowly through the lettuce and peppers on her plate.

"Death," he said, "has no explanation for them, and is thus an unacceptable thought." He squinted out into the heat haze that shimmered from the pavement across from them. "Can you imagine? An unacceptable thought? It's quite exciting, actually."

"How can it be unacceptable—to them, or anyone? They die just like everybody else."

He frowned. "It's just that belief, though, that probably invests Huascar with the power to utilize his talents—the conviction that the rest of us lack: to think the unacceptable." He continued eating for a few minutes, then went on. "The Incas believed that a man could be reborn on earth, whereupon he could then repossess all the things that had been his. This was the only way they could conceive of immortality. In some cases, a soul might possess an *illapa,* a sacred essence, quite rare, associated with only the most highly placed Incas, which was a kind of charisma that they possessed when they were alive."

"This has something to do with you, doesn't it."

"I don't know. Somehow it's all linked up. Charisma, historicity, belief, location, meteorites, Huascar... " He shrugged, then smiled.

Liana forced a return smile.

MURUROA ATOLL

22 June, 1972

The balloon rose over the horizon. McTaggart watched it, as he had each morning since its first appearance. Instead of the horror it had initially inspired, it had come to be viewed as a sign of the territorial beachhead the *Greenpeace III* had managed to establish. There was a kind of grim satisfaction to that, McTaggart felt. To hold such awesome power in check for so long was an invigorating opiate. Why else had the French navy tried to scare them off with the presence of the *De Grasse, La Bayonnaise,* and the *Hippopotame,* all maneuvering about them in blatant intimidation? It was because they were winning—temporarily, at any rate.

He smiled to himself. Weren't all victories temporary? On occasion, we all get to hold back the rush of entropy, to stem the attack of age, to stockpile against the death of love, he thought. And then it starts again. Always again.

But no matter. This moment was his, however small. The explosion had not come.

But it would. He knew that. It would come.

It always did.

LIMA, PERU
28 June, 2072

"What happens if you don't come back?"

Fletcher watched his wife's face with compassion before answering. "I'll come back."

"But what if you don't?"

"I will. Everyone has come back. There's no need to worry."

Liana was silent.

"A week. I'll be gone a week. And you'll be waiting for me, and everything will be fine." He propped himself up on one elbow and gazed down at the startling oval of his wife's face, limned against the whiteness of the pillow. Below the covers, her foot pressed against his leg.

"We have to get some sleep," he said. "It's Cuzco tomorrow. The alarm goes off at six." He reached out and stroked the black hair, soft on her pillow.

"I can't sleep."

He continued to trail his hand languidly through her hair, along the side of her face. Then she touched him, and his blood quickened.

The curtains billowed and rolled; the wind from the city's night swept in humidly, touching everything in the room with ancient rhythms. It was the same wind that slid over the stone terraces, the gabled stone and mud houses, the Andean valleys and the mountain aeries, a wind pagan and alien and feral.

In the blackness, in the silence, the curtains settled.

14

NORFOLK ISLAND
10 March, 1835

Bran Michael Dalton squinted into the glare of the noon sun at the approaching figure. The man stopped at the edge of the twenty-six foot radius, bent, and placed the bowl of food within the circle's outlined perimeter. Straightening, he glanced at Dalton, spat contemptuously, then turned on his heel and sauntered away.

Dalton ran his tongue over parched lips. Pushing himself up, he gazed at the bowl from the rim of the hollowed scoop in the earth which he had fashioned as his lair. He eyed it with a mixture of revulsion and need, the paradoxical hate one can only muster up for those things or people that give provender in bondage. The sun was high and hot, baking him with an unblinking eye.

He crawled out of his hole toward the food.

Even as he shuffled across the hardened dirt of his open prison on his hands and knees, his head down, his eyes following the scurrying of the ants in his path, he was only sure of one thing: somehow, in some unimaginable way, he was getting out of all this; he could not continue on the island. It was unthinkable.

This he vowed to himself.

17 March, 1835

"What day is it?" he called out.

The guard passing by halted and glared at him. Then he smiled and continued on, ignoring him.

Dalton watched him fade away into the shimmer of heat. It was at least ten days since anyone had spoken to him, although he had lost track.

Clutching his chain, he dropped his head back onto the sand wearily.

18 March, 1835

It was dark when he opened his eyes. Perhaps he had been awakened by some sound, perhaps it was coincidence. But the lights from the barracks provided enough illumination for him to be sure of what he saw, or at least, sure of what he thought he saw.

It was a woman.

She was standing about fifteen feet outside the twenty-six foot limit, unmoving, staring at him.

Afraid that if he moved she would leave, he lay motionless, drinking in the dim sight of her.

A woman.

She turned and left.

19 March, 1835

He saw her again the next night. This time it was not quite dark, and he had more light with which to study her. She was young, maybe eighteen, possibly twenty. Her dress was soft blue, her hair black. She seemed to be exploring the compound in a curious, aimless way. But when she saw him looking at her, she stopped and stared back.

Dalton thought that the expression on her face was one of disbelief, amazement. But there was none of the contempt that he had grown accustomed to seeing on the faces of those who came in contact with him, and this surprised him.

He had forgotten such looks. He had also managed to forget, mercifully, women, as best he could.

The stirring that he felt as he watched her was the breath of life coursing through him, and he knew, once more, what it felt like to be alive, to be a man, and it fortified him. For this he would always be grateful.

He tried smiling.

She seemed surprised, even embarrassed. Turning, she left.

He had felt strong and self-sufficient in his resolve to endure before seeing her. His eyes, now, trailed her across the compound, her form dredging up memories of a life vanished into the vast expanse of sea surrounding him. From far away and from deep within, he let the songs of his past summon him and cradle him before lapsing into the fear that accompanies true loss.

Two days later they unlocked the chain about his waist and dropped it at his feet. They told him to report to the barracks for dinner with the other prisoners. Before he left his circle, he sat down in his scooped lair one last time, a strange comfort enveloping him.

He realized that they had defiled some small part of him, because it was almost hard to leave.

15

CUZCO, PERU
30 June, 2072

Haucaypata Recreation Square, which had been renamed the Plaza de Armas in its post-Inca phase, once again languished under its illustrious, antiquated nomenclature, an honorific to the rise of the New Incas. It was, and always had been, the undisputed center of the city. The Sapi River bounded the square's southern perimeter, as it had since the city's inception, a living vein of Incan ichor which fell out of the heights that served as the city's backdrop. The indigo waters that surrounded Cuzco filled their shrine with sacred, breathing *huaca*. There had been a time when many llamas were cremated that the rivers might eat and prosper.

The great stone slabs still covered the Sapi, burying the ancient artery that linked Haucaypata with Cusipata—the Square of Leisure wedded to the Square of Joy—producing a single expanse terraced from the gully of the river by stone steps at certain places. Haucaypata itself was gilded with sifted sand, soft and pure.

Into Haucaypata, at its four corners, entered the main roads of the empire, converging on the *omphalos* with almost geometric precision, and escorting into the core the essences of a quartet of strange and far-flung *huacas*. The center of the square contained the *capac usno*, the roughly carved stone dais that was the central *huaca* of the city, the altar that was reserved for the ascension of emperors or gods or both. At its base was the stone basin, gold-holstered and hollow, the sun's maw. Toasts to the solar pater were poured into this basin, which drained into the earth, uniting the sun god and his earthbound intermediaries in the bond of family.

It was here that Fletcher Christian IV would stand. It was here that Huascar would polarize his powers.

From the window of Condorcancha, the palace of the great emperors and one of the three royal residences that surrounded Haucaypata, Christian stared down at the *usno*. That night, he would join with Huascar in washing his body in water collected from the Sapi and the Tullu, before they commingled to become the Huatanay. With such holy lavatory, sin and illness would be washed away, and he would be sanctified.

Sin and illness, he thought. They were inextricably linked for the Incas. The latter was a result of the former. The physical order stemmed from the moral order, and with this he found it hard to dissent: the visible as manifestation of the invisible. It had a conceptual harmony that appealed to him, that served his notion of a universe with a purpose.

He wondered if he was right.

He wondered if he would find out.

Tomorrow.

16

NEW ZEALAND HERALD, AUCKLAND

Thursday, 29 June, 1972

France is reported to have exploded the first nuclear device…at 11 a.m., on Monday [June 26]. News of the blast leaked out in Tahiti last night, although French officials are refusing to say anything about it…

THE SUN, VANCOUVER (PARIS-AP)

Thursday, 29 June, 1972

In Canberra, the foreign affairs department said it received a cable from the Australian Embassy in Paris saying the *Greenpeace III* was not in the danger area. It gave no other details…

THE TIMES, HAMILTON, N.Z.

Thursday, 29 June, 1972

Sounding despondent and shocked, Ann-Marie said last night's news that the protest boat's crew were in a Tahiti military hospital led her to believe *Greenpeace III* had been picked up after the blast…

WAIKATO TIMES, WELLINGTON (PA)

Thursday, 29 June, 1972

A denial that the crew of *Greenpeace III* had been detained in a French military hospital near Papeete had been made by the French Ministry of Foreign Affairs, the Prime Minister, Mr. Marshall, said in a statement today.

THE GUARDIAN, LONDON
Thursday, 29 June, 1972

... However, in the present atmosphere of uncertainty, with the fate of the crew of the ketch *Greenpeace III* still a mystery, one thing has emerged clearly on the diplomatic front: the British Government has made no protest to France this time, although protests have been made in the past, and no protests will be made when the full facts of the present explosions are made known.

In taking this decision the Prime Minister and Sir Alec Douglas-Home are consciously snubbing Australia and New Zealand, as well as Britain's SEATO partner, the Philippines. It led to sharp words from the retiring Secretary-General of SEATO, General Vargas, at the news conference in Canberra.

But these pressures will not deflect Mr. Heath and the Foreign Secretary from their policy of deferring to President Pompidou on almost all matters of high policy until Britain becomes a full member of the Common Market in January.

This strategy has now gone so far that, at the SEATO meeting, Sir Alec resisted all efforts to include a paragraph in the final communiqué criticizing the French tests. Quixotically, Sir Alec was acting on behalf of the French themselves, because President Pompidou had pointedly boycotted the Canberra meeting... The British Government is likely to find itself drawn willy-nilly into a diplomatic entanglement with France, over the fate of the *Greenpeace III*. If the crew has been injured or killed in a vessel operating in international waters where France has no legal jurisdiction, Whitehall will be drawn in to settle any claim.

Alternatively, it would appear that France has broken the international code of the sea if the reports from Tahiti—that the ketch was forcibly taken in tow by a French warship and taken to a Tahitian port—prove to be true. In law this amounts to piracy by a foreign warship.

Anthony Tucher adds: If France has exploded a nuclear device in the atmosphere, why have the monitoring systems of the watching world failed to detect it? The reasons are that the device—presumably a trigger for an H-Bomb, consists largely of Uranium-235 from Pierrelatte and beryllium reflectors—is very small, will produce only a mild atmospheric shock wave, and, since it is in the atmosphere, virtually no seismic disturbance.

The nearest non-French observers are some 500 miles from ground zero, too far away for direct monitoring. Any clues to the explosion will be fission fragments and highly irradiated residual particles which, carried up by the heat of the explosion, will be high in the atmosphere and drifting slowly across the Pacific. These will first be detected by high-flying aircraft, including those of civil airlines, many of which carry sample collectors as as a matter of routine.

It could take several days or even weeks for revealing samples to reach the various government laboratories which maintain a watch on nuclear contamination in the atmosphere…

MURUROA ATOLL
29 June, 1972
McTaggart spied a single plane, high up in the sky, circling lazily against the sun. It seemed to satisfy itself about the vessel below, then angle sharply off to the east and out of sight.

Dropping his eyes to the deck, he blinked away the effects of the brightness. The morning was brisk and clear.

"David!"

McTaggart turned toward the summons from below. It was Grant.

"Come here. Quick!"

He descended the stairs. "What is it?"

"Listen." Grant was fiddling with the radio's tuner. McTaggart recognized the voice of the announcer from Radio Australia. There was a moment of crackle, then the sound broke distinctly, if quietly:

"France is reported to have exploded a nuclear device at Mururoa Atoll at 11 a.m. Monday. The explosion was the first of a planned series for this year. News of the blast leaked out of Tahiti last night, although French officials at this time are refusing comment…"

"Monday!" Grant's eyes went wide. They stared at one another.

"Three days ago," McTaggart muttered.

"There's more…"

"… The French Government has informed Canada that the Canadian vessel *Greenpeace III* sailed out of the testing area of its own accord on June 21 and has not been seen since. The whereabouts of the vessel are not known at this time… "

McTaggart felt cold. The air about him was indeed altered, both physically and metaphysically. What the French had done was inhuman. They all felt it, in their own silent contemplation.

"Maybe the winds were in our favor," Nigel said after a while. "Maybe they took that into account. Maybe it was a small blast, and they didn't detonate until they knew we couldn't be affected."

McTaggart and Grant looked at him without speaking.

Slowly, the fear and shock were being replaced by a bitter bile. *Bastards!* McTaggart thought. *And no one on the outside knows where we are.*

Without realizing it, McTaggart found himself looking at his hands. He was surprised to see that they were steady.

17

NORFOLK ISLAND
29 June, 1835

The sty on the man's eyelid had never really abated. It was a constant, a surface pustule of the darkness that inhabited the island's soul, Dalton often thought. Yet, he had come to know the man beneath the sty, and there was consolation in that, since he was worth knowing.

Even if he was an Englishman. Percy Teversham kept his own counsel, but he was one of the few on the island whom Dalton felt he could trust.

Bent and emaciated, he was an elfin caricature, his nose too large, his chin too long. But since the day he had chanced to sit beside Bran Michael Dalton when the Irishman had been so bold as to comment on the need for a spoon and suffer the inevitable consequences, he had elevated his opinion of the stubborn Dubliner substantially. He reminded him of his baby brother, Will, back home in Liverpool, the youngest of the clan who survived and made himself heard by adopting the most outrageous bravado, and carrying it off. Will, he reflected, was still in Liverpool, eking out an existence with his wits and gall, while he, Percy, languished in this hell-hole, victim of his own timidity and bad luck.

And yet, he had never expected anything else. He had never been smart enough, like Will, to avoid the eventual snare of the law.

He had lost track of the years.

Percy felt a hand on his back, touching softly. "It's badly burned here." Dalton frowned as he inspected the sores on the man's shoulderblade.

"Fuck it."

"Yes. Fuck it." He dropped his hand and pulled even with Percy as they trudged back along the path from the barge. "Fuck the lime. Fuck the sea. Fuck the guards…"

Percy chuckled.

Dalton smiled.

The Englishman glanced at Dalton's back. "You're just as bad."

Dalton shrugged. He knew that if he could see his own back he would probably not even recognize that it was part of a human being.

"Sometimes," said Dalton, "I think flogging's more humane than a week of duty in the lime works. The sea water just loves to eat it up right off the skin."

"The trick's not to get saddled with ladin' it down to the barge. The trick's to stay at the kilns."

"The trick's how to get off this fucking island."

They were both silent for a minute, trudging with their thoughts.

"There are a lot of tricks, aren't there?"

Percy grunted.

"Too bad we're so fucking dumb we don't know any of them."

Percy chortled.

"Even a dog learns a trick or two. Why, I once saw a pig on my uncle Liam's farm that knew how to open the door of his pen, feed himself at the trough, and close the door behind him when he was through."

Shaking his head, Percy grinned madly. "You're a lyin' Irishman, Bran. You're full of the blarney, completely. There never was a pig so smart, any-where—let alone in Ireland. I mean, absolutely not in Ireland. Pigs can never be as smart as people, and in Ireland, the people don't know how to open their own doors, feed themselves, and close it behind them." He shook his head, the grin spreading.

Dalton laughed quietly. The lime burns on his own back seared with pain, eating away at the tender scar tissue that formed the major part of the surface there. He knew that it must be doubly bad for his mate, given his lack of strength, size, and health.

There were ten of them who had drawn lading duty from the kilns to the barge. Dalton and Percy Teversham brought up the rear. About forty feet ahead of them walked the lead sentry, in front of the ten prisoners. The rear guard was not yet in sight, having stayed back at the barge an extra few minutes to chat with the crew. Orange trees lined this part of the trail, their fruit beckoning, a dozen feet on either side of them.

Bran put his hand on Percy's shoulder, halting him.

"What is it?"

Dalton glanced behind them. There was no one in sight. Turning to his mate, he asked, "Want an orange?"

"You're fuckin' mad, Bran. Let's go."

Dalton stayed him with his large hand. Glancing once more about him, he bounded across the ditch, through the long grass to where the ripe fruit hung low to the ground, and in a matter of seconds, gathered half a dozen oranges in his huge paws.

"Bran!" Percy's voice wheezed the plea.

He didn't even make it back to the ditch before the rear sentry rounded the turn and stopped, staring at them. The guard's rifle rose, pointed at Dalton's chest, and a smile of malice curled about the man's lips.

Bran Michael Dalton did not move. In his hands, the oranges sat like trumpet irons, manacling him with gaudy precision. His fingers squeezed them until he pierced the fleshy rinds, sinking deeply into the juices and the sweetness.

By evening, he had received his two hundred lashes. Immediately afterward, he was escorted back to his circle of isolation, the twenty-six-foot chain locked about his waist, and left in his private prison. Pushing himself to his hands and knees, he looked around, saw the outline of his scooped-out hollow still there in the sand, and remembered its strange solace.

He crawled into it and lay there, unfeeling of anything except the pain, which was without ebb and flow, always there, like breathing. The stuff of life.

In the night, he opened his eyes without knowing why. The moonlight was streaked on the ground where it broke through the tall pines. Across the compound, standing very still, he saw her. The woman. He closed his eyes and tried to fathom her presence. When he opened them again, she was gone.

The memory of her blue dress nursed him through the pain, into exhaustion, and finally back to sleep.

The next day, by order of the commandant, the orange trees were cut down.

18

CUZCO, PERU
1 July, 2072

It was time.

Fletcher Christian IV was going into the past.

They waited until the moon had risen. This, maintained Huascar, was absolutely essential. The communion meal, the *yahuar sanco* , had been taken.

On the *usno* in the center of Haucaypata Square, Christian let his eyes wander over the sea of pageantry surrounding him. Four hundred New Incas, adorned with all the colors of the rainbow, engulfed him: one hundred on each side of the dais, facing outward toward the four corners of the Incan empire. The bonnets were festively feathered; the men wore red and white flowers, their brows silvered, their chests emblazoned with gold. The women had painted their faces, sheathed their bodies in striped garments, and pinned back flowing, jet hair with a prism of mantillas. At their breasts, silver *tupus*—shawl pins—glinted in the moonlight.

Huascar was adorned in his ceremonial, cream-colored robe, an ornate golden sun-pendant hanging on his chest, his white hair strewn with brilliant red feathers. Even in the dim light, his eyes shone with a blue fire, seeing things that others could not glimpse.

Fletcher Christian IV watched Huascar raise his hands aloft, watched him implore the Sun, the Morning Star, the Moon, the Rainbow, and Mother Earth, to unite with him in his sacred mission, to help him open the way, to bend space and time and lead through its ethereal fabric the man beside him: to unite this man with his ancestor on the island far to the west and along the great Tropic of Capricorn.

Atop the royal residences surrounding the square, the televideo units focused on the event with infra-red lenses, accompanied by argon cylinders and a battery of media reporters. Huascar's insistence on the absence of unnatural lighting, on using only the wan light of the moon, was being dealt with in modern fashion—in stark contrast to the spectacle it was capturing.

At the window of the Condorcancha, Fletcher fixed his eyes upon Liana, who stood where she had remained for the past two hours, unmoving. She was, he realized again, his rock, the only real thing he could focus on amid the ocean of exotic color, scent, and taste that was consuming him.

Her gaze did not waver.

The ceremonial fires were cleansing the air throughout the city, their auras flickering spectrally against the darkening sky. The purification was almost complete.

Fletcher found himself at the center of a haunting canopy of riotous color. He wanted to believe. And amidst the spectacle, he found it hard not to.

Huascar spoke aloud. The words were simple, hypnotic, a croon to gods and powers that rode the swelling updrafts that swirled about the Andean steeps.

"Hear me. Where art thou? Within? Without? In shadow? In cloud? Light the way through the funnel of Time, to our past, to our memory, to our destiny. Hear me. Respond. Be our guide."

The ancient mystic's weathered, leathery face virtually glowed with an ardor and a passion that transcended his body. His eyes, unblinking, were focused on some invisible point in the darkness. His hands remained aloft, palms outward.

A wind sprang up.

The sand at the foot of the *usno* eddied. The wind was a song, a canticle from beyond time; part vesper, part hymn, part dirge.

Fletcher shivered.

There were ghosts about him everywhere. He could feel it. The past was all ghosts. They were coming. Huascar was summoning them.

The moon flowed over him, its beauty branding him like fire and ice. Huascar's chant rose and fell, rhythms like the tides.

Fletcher saw the words hanging in the air before his eyes like jewels on a golden necklace, each one a talisman, shimmering and radiant.

Besides the stone basin at the foot of the *usno* a procession of women came forth to offer libation to the gods, pouring wines and sacred water into the golden receptacle, the fluids dissipating into the sands of the square, into the earth that was bound to the sun. Their movement was as rhythmic as the chant, their colors as hypnotic.

On the basin's opposite side, in the dignity of death, was the mummy bundle of Huascar's predecessor, its gold-plated and empty visage gazing vacantly over the throng that it had once ruled imperiously. The mummy's daughter, very much alive, stood by its side, her face painted a wild vermilion, her expression otherworldly.

Fletcher felt himself being absorbed into something large. Something that was growing larger.

The air about him changed. The difference was magnetic, powerful. He became light-headed.

Huascar's chant continued.

Fletcher's head began to swim. He felt like he was—he searched for the word—*evaporating.*

Again, he shivered convulsively, his body tingled, as if an electric current was disseminating his very atoms.

He could not see his feet. Nor could he feel them. *Evaporating.*

Huascar intoned his invocation. The chant throbbed through his being. The crowd surrounding them began to sway. Torches lit the night on the square—tongues of flame, sinuous in the gathering dark.

Fire that cleansed.

Fletcher felt pushed from within. *Pushed.* It welled up from depths he had never known, beyond the lowest point of his physical body, above the apex of his brain.

Pushed.

He felt his consciousness spin into a gyre of wind and white light, a vortex of the Peruvian night that had yawed wide to swallow him.

Then, without warning, he felt the rivers of the Empire flow through his soul, converge into a cataract that siphoned through his being, washing him along with its pull, bearing him downstream, over the precipice…

Plummeting

Down

Back

His hands were gone.

"Oh memory, oh loss, within, without. Help us. Take him. Through Time."

A needle tossed into a maelstrom, his consciousness ballooned from within. The pageant around him became cuttingly clear, yet remotely distant—a discarded frame on an ancient roll of film. In stop-action, he watched the *usno* fade in jerked sequences, each one wrenching him farther from the heart of the ceremony, each visual fading until there was only the haunting, silver moon pouring light into his universe, a universe that had ceased to be tangible, ceased to have form.

He flowed like water. Along Time's river.

Back.

In Haucaypata Square the crowd hushed and turned in unison to stare at the *capac usno*. Fletcher Christian IV was no longer there.

Placing his hands against his forehead, Huascar saw him.

In his mind's eye.

In the void.

19

MURUROA ATOLL

1 July, 1972

At 0830 hours, McTaggart heard it, a sound he never wanted to hear: a muffled growl, too loud to be the wind, more like the onset of a storm, ripping across the leaden sky. Then he felt it, a vibration that shook the deck of the *Greenpeace III,* shook the very fiber of his soul.

There was no doubt. France had done it.

Exploded the bomb.

With them there.

The rumble lasted eight seconds, then died. Nigel and Grant both came up on deck. No one spoke.

Unable to see it in the sky, unable to confirm what they knew, they denied it with silence.

McTaggart looked up. There were no birds. There was nothing.

Within minutes the ketch was under sail. The primal instinct was to flee, however impossible, from what they knew was now rolling toward them: the insane wind that boiled with apocalyptic madness, crested with nature's seething imbalance.

It was there: in the wind, in the sky, in their hearts, in their minds. McTaggart thought of his children.

There seemed to be only the past.

The future had disappeared. And everything had changed. Even as McTaggart watched over his shoulder, he knew it. It wasn't just his life that had shifted, but everything.

Everything.

Destinies, dreams, hopes, perceptions—all transmuted forever in the glacial weight of the bomb.

Paths altered. Forever.

His skin prickled. He was not the same. The bomb had done it. It had torn open the sky, torn open his soul, warped everything.

In his head, he heard the screams of lost souls, felt the dread of people displaced, sensed the confusion of mortal transubstantiation.

Something incredible had happened.

Something that fouled Time, the very structure of the linear universe.

He sailed on through the night, knowing that the wind at his back came from a hole in the very nature of things.

* * * * *

Fletcher Christian IV and Huascar had encountered a force that dwarfed both them and their plans.

The Bomb.

20

1 July, 2072

Fletcher Christian IV floated where there was nothing. He had lost everything: body, world, Liana. The cataract that swept him along fired his being with a wave of sparks.

He was going back. He could feel it. *Back.*

The trajectory was something he could see, like an immense tunnel down which he was being drawn, as if by a magnet, the route clear.

Then, without warning, the side of the tunnel appeared to rupture. The force that burst through deafened him, engulfed him, then pulled him down sideways as it retreated into the gaping rent it had created.

Without knowing how or why, he knew that what was happening was *wrong.* This was not the route. *Something had gone wrong.*

The force, the power that took him with it, was awesome.

There was no escaping its clutches; its strength and pull were relentless, unpitying.

But the image that flashed through whatever consciousness he still maintained was one that he recognized totally. Everyone knew it. It was one of mankind's new primal images, born in the twentieth century, living forever: the mushroom cloud, its cap a maelstrom that unfolded like a demented geyser, even here, in this tributary of Time, pulling him sidewise.

Changing everything.

1 July, 1835

In his hole, chained to his rock, Bran Michael Dalton lay stretched out on his back, his arms turned palm outward. The moon bathed him with quicksilver, but did not heal. His eyes were open, staring into the night, but the only thing they saw was his past. They strained and hunted the pitch above him, but there was no future, nothing to see. It would end, he thought, here, on Norfolk. Perhaps here, in this hole.

What had happened? How had it happened? Dublin. *A memory. Another. A fragment, an image.* Sweet Mary. His Da. Gone.

And yet, it was all there was, this fractured past, this jumble of broken tiles.

The moon disappeared. From nowhere, a wind sprang up, softly at first, then aboil with unnatural anger. Cold enveloped him, seizing him with a tight fist, squeezing him until he became afraid.

He raised his head, out of both fear and curiosity. The wind, a force he could neither see nor understand, beat at him furiously.

His legs, he saw, were disappearing. Then his waist.

Terror gripped him. *I'm going fucking mad,* he thought. *I'm dying. I must be.*

Suddenly, in his mind, the wind took shape, a form of which he had no previous knowledge: a giant waterspout of boiling air and water, overflowing at its crown into a dark cloud of horror that fed upon itself, drifting angrily across a sky he had never seen before, its flat body stalking the horizon, blackening any light.

He put his hand to his face, but he had no hand. He had no face either, he realized.

Yet he could still think, after a fashion. And he could still *feel.* It was easy to conclude that he had died, and that he would soon meet his maker. For a moment, his fear battled his obstinacy, and he wondered if he should tell God what a stinking mess He had left behind Him after those first seven days.

1 July, 2072

Huascar stopped his chant. His eyes opened. About him, the assembly hushed.

Those who previously had been privy to the rite knew that something was amiss. All eyes turned to Huascar.

His face was the face of a man who has suffered a horror beyond explication, who has seen a truth so unsettling that he is momentarily not with the living.

They waited.

A full minute passed. Huascar's face remained a lined chart into unknown horror. Finally, he spoke. Softly.

"I've lost him."

The words were breathed with despair and incredulity upon the crowd.

"He's gone."

He spoke so quietly that Liana, at the window of the Condorcancha, gazing down upon the spectacle, was unable to pick up the words. Nevertheless, she knew what he had said. Everyone knew.

The air, so alive mere minutes before, was an iron slab, a generator with the power switched off.

A streak of nightcloud cut the moonlight into ragged peaks upon the sands at their feet.

"He's gone," he repeated. "Into Time."

He lowered his head. At his side, at his back, at his feet, everyone waited.

"Something took him," he said.

No one understood.

"Something awful," he added. But even he did not understand. Nor would anyone.

III

The splitting of the atom has changed everything,
save our mode of thinking…

— Albert Einstein

Such is the uneven state of human life;
and it afforded me a great many curious speculations afterwards,
when I had a little recovered my first surprise.

— Daniel Defoe, *Robinson Crusoe*

21

NORFOLK ISLAND
1 July, 1835

Fletcher Christian IV thought that he must have blacked out momentarily. There was a gap in his consciousness, followed by a flare of light and dark in instant succession, of pressure and release, and then the return of tactile sensation, like the tingling of fingers and toes thawing from the cold. Air filled his lungs, and he drank it deeply, trying not to gasp, its wonderful purity convincing him that he was indeed alive after all.

He was on his hands and knees. Beneath his fingers, hard earth and sand told him that he was very much outdoors, as did the smells of the air about him, rife with the scents of pine, grass, and dew.

He blinked. It was night. Through the sweat that stung the edges of his eyes, white moonlight filtered into his vision, and he blinked again, trying to focus.

And then he remembered. Everything. The full moon hanging in the sky above him, haunting and cold, seemed to pour into his brain, illumining his memory, like pages in an album flipped slowly backward.

The usno. *The fires beckoning in the night. The chanting.*

And then he recalled the monstrous presence that had obtruded as he was arcing through time. *The mushroom cloud. A nuclear bomb, explod-*

ing, terrible in its power and fury, tearing through the very fabric of time and space and hurling about everything in its range with demented rage.

He had been a straw in a nuclear wind, a wind that condenses matter to its elemental units, and then disperses them with shattering autocracy. Yet he had survived. Somehow. And for him, this was a matter of some wonder, for even without full comprehension of the particulars, he nevertheless understood the extent of the force that had toyed with him, however briefly.

Perhaps the vision of the explosion was a routine part of the temporal transmission. But as soon as he entertained the notion, he dismissed it, for on its heels stumbled Christian's recollection of the *wrongness* of its intrusion. Its presence had been a mistake. He had felt it.

This, he though, *must be Pitcairn. I made it! I survived, and am in the past.* His chest swelled with the euphoria of the idea, of having pierced Time itself, the most relentless of all forces, the shaper of history, identity, the midwife of pain and joy on a scale both so vast and so minute that Time itself was a god, a god maddeningly mindless and omnipotent.

Until lately.

Until Huascar, and man in general, had found its fallibility, its entrypoint, and probed with tentative, tiny fingers, for its heart. And he had been a part of it. Christian could scarcely believe his fortune—he was actually here. *Pitcairn.* His ancestors' destiny, and now, his. It humbled him to have eked out a place in the shape of things.

He tried to move and was puzzled by the weight at his waist. Touching his hand there, he felt the cold of the steel links, the heft of its inert presence, and with both of his hands now, he found himself tracing the outline of the substantial chain with increasingly apprehensive fingers. And then he saw its dead outline coiling along the ground away from him, a sleeping python, quiet in the moonlight, in whose embrace he appeared to be snared. Slowly, his joy faded, and he felt the beginnings of a deep and true fear.

22

PITCAIRN ISLAND
1 July, 1972

Bran Michael Dalton was certain that he had been taken by the devil him-self, a demonic force and presence so frightening that he wondered why God would create an afterlife for His creatures that could encompass such a horrific possibility. Father Garrett, back in Dublin, had warned him. Even that Protestant minister who skulked among the men on Norfolk had told them about the consequences of sin. Now, he wished he had heeded them. He wished that he had had a chance to confess before dying. A fluttering of memories and religious images from his childhood paraded through his stunned consciousness, all of them unsettling in a different way.

It seemed to have stopped.

He was lying on his side. Gradually, the feeling returned to his limbs, spreading methodically throughout the rest of his body. With this, Dalton experienced a mixture of confusion and relief—confusion as to what had happened, and relief that he apparently was not dead.

At least he didn't feel dead. And he thought that being dead would somehow be much more different from being alive than seemed to be the case.

He rolled over and pushed up onto his knees, his eyes wide. It was night, but the moon still shone brightly.

He had no idea where he was.

It took him more than a minute to experience the next stage of emotions. It took him that long to discover that his chain was gone, that he was free, and with the realization, his heart soared.

And although he was afraid that it was all a dream, a hoax, some way in which God was playing with him, he still could not contain his joy, so powerful and uncontrollable was it as it surged up from the depths of his being. He let it flow over him, bathing him in the solace that he had ceased contemplating could ever exist for him again. Trembling, he stood erect, his knees weak, in the night, in the moonlight, in the terrible, wonderful dark of the world that enveloped him in its mystery, that had somehow given him this miraculous second chance at life, freed him for he knew not what.

And yet, he distrusted it. It was his nature. Everyone he knew distrusted anything that appeared too easily. The sensibility was a firm brick in the foundations built in the slums of Dublin, a survival mechanism, imbuing its recipients with a wariness that often kept them from being the fool, often kept them alive.

Hope and fear waged their silent battle within him. He had not forgotten the monstrous presence that had summoned him into the void, catapulting him here—wherever "here" was.

But he was free. That was the upshot of it all. Dead or alive, heaven or hell or somewhere else, he was free. And standing there, he found himself crying, then sobbing, as his mind tried to grasp what was ungraspable, for with the freedom came the loss of everything he had known, again. As it always came to him.

As it always would.

23

NORFOLK ISLAND
1 July, 1835

Christian stood up, bewildered. He gazed into the darkness, trying for bearings of any kind. Unable to make out anything of significance in the limited light cast down by the moon, he began to take up the slack of the chain that girded his waist, following it to its mooring around the boulder that seemed to be his anchor. It told him nothing.

Except that he was a prisoner.

This was enough, in many ways. It confirmed his gut feeling that things were definitely not as they should be; in fact, it lent credibility to the overpowering intuition he had that not only were *things* not as they should be, neither were *places.*

It didn't feel like Pitcairn, nor like 1972, and he couldn't put his finger on why.

He tested the length of his tether by striding to its limit. *I'm a dog on a goddamn leash,* he thought. Walking slowly, his eyes straining into the darkness all the while, he completed the three hundred and sixty degrees that was his most expansive path, and felt little wiser for doing so. There were moments of near panic, quelled by the inquiring mind of the scientist investigating yet another puzzle. But Christian was no fool, and he was beginning to be seriously worried. *Where am I? What should I do? And why, for God's sake, am I chained, like some goddamn leper or madman?*

At the last thought, he halted and straightened. *Maybe,* he thought, *I am mad. Maybe I've gone crazy. Maybe I've always been crazy, always been chained here, and only now gained enough sanity to discover this.* Then he realized that he was courting true madness by even entertaining such a thought, shook his head, and concentrated once more on deciding what he should do as a course of first action. He stared off into the night, squinting hard. As he did so, his eyes gradually adjusted, and the night-shapes of trees and shrubbery began to become apparent. And in the distance, he saw what might be a building of some sort. It was possible, he thought. He squinted again. Perhaps a low bunker of some kind. Did they have such things on Pitcairn in 1972? He didn't think so, but couldn't be sure. He couldn't be sure of anything, he realized with a wry sense of grimness.

What should I do?

Suddenly, he did it.

"Hello!" The two syllables rang out across the compound, echoing into the damp night, silencing the songs of crickets. He waited a moment, then added, "Is anybody there?" Again, the question was shouted at full volume, and left a diminishing series of haunting reverberations in the stillness.

A man appeared, shambling toward him out of the shadows. His presence gave Christian a start, filling him with both anticipation and apprehension, for he was quick to note his dress. The worn and muddied leather boots, the bulky and ill-fitting woolen coat, and not least of all, the antiquated firearm—a rifle of some sort—that he gripped in his hand, were all clues to Christian that this was not 1972. His confusion, though, was at bay temporarily in the presence of another human being. At least I'm not alone, he thought. Wherever I am.

For a moment they stared at one another.

Christian's next words were spoken crisply, carefully, and softly. "Good evening, sir. I'm afraid there's been some mistake." He gestured to the chain at his waist. "If you'd be good enough to unlock this—" he held the padlock at his waist in his fingers, "then I'm sure we'd both benefit greatly from a sharing of information." He then offered his hand in friendship. "I'm Fletcher Christian IV." His hand remained outstretched, waiting, hoping to clasp the hand of the man before him, his only thought being that common sense had to prevail here eventually.

The man's face slowly turned sour. When he spoke, it was with both anger and contempt.

"You're a fuckin' madman, Dalton." He paused, then spat at Christian, who recoiled in shock. "Be quiet. If you wake anyone up at the house, you'll spend the rest of your fuckin' life right here, outdoors, like the fuckin' animal you are."

Christian stood, gaping, his mind spinning through an endless skein of possibilities, none of which made sense. And then there was the fear— the very real fear—that he may do or say something that would further jeopardize his position, whatever that position was. Yet he couldn't accept that this man was unable to see that he was someone other than whom he had addressed—this Dalton, whoever he may be.

Then the man looked at him more closely, frowning. "Where'd you get them clothes?"

Christian glanced down at himself, startled. He looked back at the man confronting him. "They're mine. I'm not Dalton." He licked his lips, waiting.

The man squinted at him, peering carefully. A fly buzzed in his brain, slowly and irritatingly, then faded. Finally, he spat once more in Christian's direction, this time aiming at his feet. "Lie down and shut up, you silly bastard." He turned to leave.

"Wait!"

The man turned on his heel, glowering now.

"You can't leave me like this!" Both hands were out now, imploring.

The rifle shifted in the man's grip, tilting upward menacingly.

Christian noted its increased prominence with wary eyes.

"Where am I?"

The man frowned.

"Why am I here?"

The man eyed him with calculated smugness now "You're nowhere, Dalton. Like always. Nowhere. And you know why?" Christian stared back at him silently.

"Because you're an arsehole. That's why you're here, Dalton. That's why everyone's here." He spat toward Christian, who this time did not even flinch. "We're all arseholes. In nowhere." Then he glared at Christian for a moment. "But you," he said, "you're the biggest arsehole of all!" A half-smile of sick amusement played at the corner of his mouth. "You're the one with the chain. Not me."

The man turned to leave once more.

"Don't leave. Not yet."

This time, when the man turned to face Christian, there was only the ugliness on his face. He raised his weapon and pointed it at Christian. "Maybe I'll tell them you tried to attack me. Tell 'em that you went fuckin' mad. I think you have gone fuckin' mad, Dalton." He paused. "Not another sound. You understand?"

Christian made no response.

This seemed to infuriate the man, who took four long steps into the radius of Christian's circle and with a quick lift of his leg kicked Christian full in the stomach. Completely surprised and suddenly winded, Christian fell backward onto the ground, clutching his stomach, gasping for breath, his eyes beginning to water.

"You understand?" The man was screaming at him now, his rage glowing from him like a beacon.

Christian said nothing. He was unable to pull enough air into his lungs to breathe properly, let alone to utter a response of any kind.

The man standing above him seemed appeased by his silence,

interpreting it as acquiescence, and the heavy breathing that accompanied the outburst of temper began to subside. But he was unable to resist one last kick into Christian's side, sending further shock waves of pain streaming through the scientist's crumpled body.

Only then did the man turn and leave.

On the ground, in shock and pain and fear, Fletcher Christian IV tried to make sense of what was happening. The only thing he understood, though, was that he was in the biggest trouble of his life, and that there might be no way out. This notion remained a constant throughout the long night, as he awaited the morning, to see what a new day might bring.

But he waited with more dread than hope.

With the dawning light, Christian was able to see his surroundings. He had not slept at all. There had been a period of time in the night that was akin to sleep in that he was scarcely conscious of his physical self; it was the type of stupor not unlike that induced by shock. In truth, it was probably a form of shock, and the body's way of enduring the trauma was to comatize the mind temporarily. He could not remember the exact moment he had emerged from this state, the faint light of morning turning the edge of the sky yellow and orange. But it was with sudden recognition of the altered light and the transformed sounds—crickets replaced by starlings and gulls—that he pulled himself from the depths of his withdrawal and examined his new milieu.

He pushed himself to his feet, swaying groggily, trying to control his faculties. The sun was rising rapidly over the treetops, most of which were tall, elegant pines. He was where he had thought: nowhere, chained to a rock, with a locomotive radius of about seven or eight meters. The building he thought he had seen in the night was indeed there: a low, stone bunker of some sort. It resembled an army barracks from a bygone era, he thought: and then realized that it might be just that.

Beyond it, elevated on a green mound of manicured lawn, was a mansion of not insignificant proportions. Christian squinted, searching for detail. Affronting the stately house was a cannon, resplendent and shining in the pale light. Christian wondered whether it was functional or merely decorative; his encounter with the man in the night with the primitive weapon told him that it may very well be functional, depending on where and when he had arrived.

The thought brought it all back. *Where and when am I?* And the strange reaction of the man he had encountered warned him that there may be no easy extrication from this *where* and *when*.

In the midst of this thought he noticed the barred windows on the mansion.

Still assimilating this data, he paced off the widest arc possible. Gazing off in the opposite direction, he could see a large quadrangle and more barracks some half-mile distant. There were other buildings scattered about at sparse intervals, and behind them all, the sea, quiet now, stretching on as only it can, beyond the eye and the mind.

The place had the feel of an island, Christian thought. Nothing definite. Just a feeling, perhaps a smell. Something about the way the clouds hung in the sky, the way they moved—rapidly and lightly—that was characteristic of all the islands he had known.

He frowned, taking in the data of sight, sound, and smell. A range of theories flitted through his brain, but he refused to give any of them more weight than any other in the absence of more verifiable fact.

Returning to the rock at the center of his circle, he seated himself and waited for those who inhabited this place to rise and get on with their day. Wait and see, he thought. Given his experience in the night, it seemed the wisest thing to do.

He hoped he was right.

PITCAIRN ISLAND
1 July, 1972

Lisa Christian's dreams were, to a great extent, the dreams of every eighteen-year-old girl. She idled away hours fantasizing about boys, cars, clothes, music, and boys again. The difference was that for Lisa, they were all too apt to remain just that: dreams. And she knew it.

For what difference did it make what she wanted or what she dreamed of having? On an island as isolated as Pitcairn, with a population of eighty-five, Fletcher Christian I's lithesome descendant might just as well wish for a castle of her own in Adamstown as expect her fair share of choice when it came to boys, cars, clothes, music, and boys again.

And for the past year this fact had been sinking in with a vengeance. Why, there hadn't even been a new house built on the island since old Pervis finished his back in 1953. A career? Marriage? She had to chuckle at the futility of it all.

Lisa remembered her summer in New Zealand two years ago with increased longing. True, it had been unbearably smelly, and the water had been disgustingly treated with something awful to enable so many people to drink it. But it had offered excitement on a level that was entirely new to her, and she reveled in the memories.

She was the only Pitcairner who wore jewelry. Silver glinted against her long, brown Polynesian neck like the moon on the night waters of Bounty Bay. And her long, coffee-colored legs flashed out of a mini-skirt that she had sewn after seeing the latest styles in a magazine from New Zealand, left behind by one of the last supply ships. She loved the new fashions. She was pretty, and she knew it; and she knew that a pretty girl needed pretty clothes to be *really* pretty.

Lisa could never be accused of not having a good sense of herself. She had even got "engaged" to John Powell, the RAF technician who had been stationed on the island last April. They had pledged their love on the third night he was on Pitcairn; he had remained for two months. Then he had been recalled to England. Lisa wrote to the address he gave her, and waited for him to write for six months before realizing that what she had feared was in fact the case. She had hurled her imitation topaz ring far out into the bay a short while later.

John Powell had not been her first lover, but on some days, Lisa feared he might be her last—or at least, the last she might truly want. That summer in Wellington she had experimented profusely with sex, and had mastered the fine points that had eluded her with her choice of partners here on Pitcairn. The men of Wellington put the boys of Pitcairn to shame.

The elders of Pitcairn regarded sex from a much more Polynesian point-of-view than their English ancestors. In a community that had none of the modern entertainments, such as films, organized sports, school dances, shops, or even TV, what was one expected to do in the evenings? A Pitcairn girl could return from a "date" at dawn with never a question from her parents. The young regarded it all as inevitable and natural—something to grow into. In such a relatively prurient society, sexual ethics remained a curious paradox, small testimony to some of the results of a culture in isolation.

And like all Pitcairn teens, she had a good supply of condoms in her bag. She had heard a lot about the Pill, especially in Wellington, but the problem of assuring a continuous supply of such drugs was too substantial to be overcome as yet.

Lisa was pondering all this and more—her future, or lack of same—as she headed down to the pool off the Edge, ostensibly to catch some crayfish; in reality merely a chance for distraction by cavorting in the blue waters there. Underneath her frilly pink top and minuscule skirt, she wore a scanty print bikini. While propelling beneath the churning waters, she was quite often overtly admired by the males in the vicinity, and Lisa courted such attention, even though she knew it wouldn't lead to anything significant. Nevertheless, it was all she had, and this was not to be dismissed out of hand.

She was lucky that day. She managed to snare three six-pounders. With each one, she waded ashore and tossed it in the gunny sack. Her wet suit clung to her curves like the trade winds caressing the palm trees.

* * * * *

Amid the scent of the jasmine, and surrounded by the softness of the hibiscus and the palms, Bran Michael Dalton watched the creature from the recesses of his erotic imagination slink in and out of the surf, occasionally surfacing from the blue water with an enormous crayfish in her grip. Christ Almighty Jesus Mary and Joseph, he thought. What a beauty! It was an additional puzzle to mull over. Where am I? He had heard of places like Pago Pago, or Bora Bora. This must be one of them, he concluded. It sure as hell wasn't Norfolk, that was certain.

He watched the girl swimming and diving in the pool sheltered from the harsher swell of the sea by a jetty of natural coral—watched her with a silence that was almost reverential, from his own secluded position amid long fronds and tall grass skirting the beach. He had only been there a matter of minutes when this walking vision had appeared, doffed the tiniest skirt Dalton could ever imagine, and began to sport practically naked right before his eyes in the water.

Her black hair, wet and straight, framed a face and mouth so sensuous that Dalton felt the stirrings of desire even before he felt any apprehension. And her eyes, he thought. Look at them. Pools as brown as a dun cow in Meath. And a waist that a man could seize in both hands...

Dalton had ceased thinking about women for good reason. It was too frustrating. Still, he was a man, and the memories and desires came flooding back without missing a beat. In fact, due in great measure to the length of his abstinence, the flood threatened to become a cataract quite easily. Dalton tried to get himself under control, and succeeded modestly. Still shaky though, and stunned at this latest addition to the spate of new data that was deluging him, he remained out of sight. *What to do?*

Right about then, the girl glanced up at his hiding place, staring hard. Then a mischievous smile played about her full lips, and her eyes danced a step or two.

Dalton crouched lower behind the foliage.

The girl then placed her hands on her hips and thrust her shoulders back, arching her breasts forward provocatively. It was not the first time that the boys had hidden in the grass to catch a glimpse of her, she thought. And she didn't mind at all. Any excitement was welcome in the solemn community of Pitcairn, and Lisa was as stifled as any healthy teenager would be in such an environment. Perhaps even more, for there was something of the minx about her. In Auckland or Wellington or Sydney, she'd have given a father a breakdown trying to keep an eye on her escapades with the opposite sex.

She shifted her weight onto one foot, bending her right knee coyly. Then she laughed aloud.

Dalton became frightened.

"I see you up there!" she called out.

Dalton remained hunched over, furiously trying to make the right decision.

"Warren? Or is it Michael? Or Tom?" She shielded her eyes and peered intently.

Dalton began to sweat. Get a hold of yourself, he thought. She's no more than a girl. She can't hurt you.

He wished he knew where he was. Then, he thought, I'd know what to do.

He was afraid again. Fear was becoming the only thing he felt he really understood.

When the stranger stood up out of the grass and stepped forward, Lisa Christian was properly startled. She had no idea who he was. Strangers to Pitcairn were always well-announced—even heralded—before their arrival on the island, for there was no way that anyone could arrive without attention.

Few places in the world were as out of the way of regular air service or shipping lines as Pitcairn—places with as much history, intrigue, or tropical climate, at any rate. Even the Galapagos drew regular tourists; Easter Island had forged a link with Santiago via twice-weekly jetliners. But when anyone inquired at a local travel agency about the possibility of visiting Pitcairn, the answers varied from a puzzled frown, to a shrug of the shoulders, to "impossible," or finally, perhaps, to the only real determinants: "How badly do you want to get there? How much are you willing to spend?"

The island had no airstrip. The harbor was inaccessible. Private yacht charter, the only reasonable answer, remained an intricate and expensive solution.

Strangers were unheard of, unthought of.

Lisa had no frame of reference for discovering the man she had never seen before staring down at her here on Pitcairn. And for this reason, partially, she had none of the fear or natural caution that any other girl in any other setting might have felt; the rest of the reason was simply that she was Lisa -confident, self-assured, pretty, and wily.

Crayfish and the latest fashions—all were instantly forgotten.

He was a tall man, broad-shouldered, with dark, curly hair and a bushy black beard. His only clothing appeared to be the pair of woolen trousers that he wore, ragged at the knees, and beltless. Through all the filth and grime that covered his flesh, though, Lisa was astute enough to make out the frame and bearing of a fine specimen of manhood, all the shabby externals notwithstanding. It was as though he had fallen from the sky, she thought. And if he had, she wasn't going to let the opportunity slip through her fingers.

A man—an outsider—a good-looking man, here, on Pitcairn. She saw the possibilities at once.

"I'm Lisa," she said, enhancing it with a smile of teeth like pearls.

The man stood before her, some thirty feet distant, and actually began to wring his hands together. He started to speak, then halted, licked his lips, and darted his eyes about, conveying an obvious nervousness. But he did not move toward her; there was nothing in his carriage or gesture to threaten her. He seemed genuinely confused, and Lisa was all the more puzzled by him. How long had he been on Pitcairn? Where had he been living? Had he jumped ship from some passing steamer? A castaway? Lisa's mind sifted a number of possibilities. It occurred to her that he may be a madman, but even if that were so, she knew she could deal with it, given the distance between them and her own natural aptitude for swimming. The sea was, after all, right at her back. He could be no true menace.

"Do you understand English?" she asked.

This time, after a few seconds, the man nodded. Encouraged, she added, "What's your name?"

The man stepped forward a pace, to the edge of the sand, ran a hand through his matted, long hair, pulling it back from his face. His eyes, she saw, were piercing blue, but they did not radiate the turbulence of madness; instead, they yielded a helplessness that he was unable to mask.

She took a step forward. Hesitantly, she tried again. "Your name?" He was, she thought, truly good-looking, and stood a good six feet in height.

She liked tall men.

"Dalton," he said, suddenly.

Lisa Christian's long eyelashes batted with surprise at the word.

"Bran Michael Dalton."

They stood without speaking, staring at each other. "Where am I?" the man asked.

Lisa listened to the accent. He was not from around here. She had heard the accent somewhere before—perhaps on TV, or at the movies—but could not place it. It lilted and rolled for her with mystery and music.

"Pitcairn," she said.

He frowned.

"You're on Pitcairn Island."

He continued to frown.

"How did you get here?" she asked. "Did you fall off a ship?"

"I don't know," he said. "I don't know where Pitcairn Island is either."

"There's only one Pitcairn Island. You mean you've never heard of it?"

He shook his head.

"Have you never heard of *Mutiny on the Bounty?*"

When he shook his head this time, Lisa became more puzzled than ever. Everyone had heard of *Mutiny on the Bounty* somehow, somewhere. It was the island's claim to fame. It was *her* claim to fame. It never failed to get a response—usually one of amazement and delight from outsiders. Captain Bligh and Fletcher Christian had entered into popular mythology: novels, films, even cartoons. Could the man be dazed or was he just in shock?

"Is Pitcairn in the Pacific?" he asked suddenly.

When Lisa nodded in the affirmative, he seemed to relax for the first time. At least, she thought, he's heard of the Pacific.

Dalton felt himself become more composed. At least I'm in the Pacific, he thought. And I don't think I'm dead now—definitely not. In fact, I feel more alive than I have in ages.

He eyed the lovely girl before him, still unable to come to terms with what seemed such astounding and inexplicable fortune. The salt water of the ocean was drying on her skin, leaving a lustrous sheen of health and beauty. He felt the soft trade winds on his own chest and arms as he studied the tiny scraps of cloth covering the girl's breasts and hips—a bright green print with pink flowers splashed randomly about. It dazed him merely to contemplate it all.

"What's Pitcairn near?" he asked.

The girl giggled. "It's not near anything."

The silence was back between them as he tried to determine how to pursue this. "I mean," he asked, "what's the nearest land, the nearest country?"

"Depends. You could say we're near Tahiti, but we're not really—not unless you think 1200 miles is near. Or you could say New Zealand is the nearest country, but that's more than twice as far. So you see, it's like I said—we're not really near anything." Her dark brown eyes twinkled.

Dalton nodded, beginning to understand. Tahiti he had heard of. And New Zealand was closer to Norfolk than was Australia. He had some bearings at last. But how in the name of blazes did I get here?

"Where did you come from?" she asked.

Dalton studied her, trying to decide what he should tell her. Finally, he told her the truth as he knew it. "I'm not sure," he said. "I'm not at all sure."

⋆ ⋆ 25 ⋆ ⋆

NORFOLK ISLAND
2 July, 1835

With the stirrings of life around him, Fletcher Christian IV felt the onset of an impatience that he had to master. If he acted rashly, as he would have liked to have done, he sensed that he would pay for it both in the short and the long run. This was a situation that he was going to have to play by ear, and one that he would have to play very carefully.

He hefted the chain in his right hand.

Men were pouring forth from the stone barracks that he had first spotted in the night. Soldiers. The routine activities of the day were commencing.

In the other direction, there was also a stirring of morning life. He noticed now what he had failed to note, somehow, earlier: that this barracks and its surrounding buildings all sported barred windows. And when men emerged from it, it was always in a group of ten or twenty, with one or two soldiers acting as guards.

This, along with his own plight, told him much.

He was in a prison of some kind.

Perhaps he was in the middle of a war—perhaps it was a military prison. But he could recall no war with a prison camp of this size on what appeared to be a tropical island, with English-speaking populace in dress that seemed at least mid-Victorian.

The puzzle knotted tighter, even as it revealed itself detail by detail.

He had to get somebody's attention. Yet it was more than obvious that he was being ignored—by everyone. And recalling his attempt to get attention in the night, he remained doubly uncertain how he should go about it.

As he pondered the dilemma, two soldiers headed in his direction, one of them carrying a small bucket. He watched them with anticipation as they crossed the open space between the military barracks and his circle. When they got close enough, he was able to see that neither of them was the man who had assaulted him in the night, and he felt relief, and some hope.

He walked halfway to the edge of his circle and stood waiting.

They ambled up to the edge of the circle and placed the bucket within his reach. Food, he thought. It must be food. Of course.

When they turned and left without speaking, he experienced a ripple of panic. They couldn't leave yet, he thought. I have to achieve some sort of sensible contact with these people. There's no other way.

"Hello there!"

The two soldiers stopped in their tracks, looked at each other, then turned slowly about to stare back at the prisoner.

"There's been some mistake." He held the chain out like an offering. "I'm not Dalton," he said, using the name he had gotten from his nighttime assailant. "I'm Fletcher Christian IV. I shouldn't be here."

The larger man stared at him open-mouthed. Something *did* seem different. The fly circled lazily in his brain. He looked at his partner then back at Christian before taking a step toward him.

"I'd like to speak with your commanding officer. Would you pass the request on to him?"

The men were dumbfounded. The closer one spoke after shaking his head in disbelief. "You must *like* bein' flogged, Dalton." He continued shaking his head. "I can't fuckin' believe even you're as dumb as this."

"He's Irish," his companion said. "That should explain it." A hoot of contempt followed.

Still staring at him, the larger man added, "I think I'll perform an act of Christian charity and forget I heard you say anything. Your memory is shorter than the space between your ears."

The other man laughed as they turned to leave.

Real panic started to set in now as Christian felt them withdrawing. He was torn between knowing that they might brutalize him as the man in the night had done, for any or no reason at all, and knowing if they went away, he would be no further ahead. He would remain a prisoner here until he could get somebody to pay attention to him so that he could tell his story—whatever they might believe.

But that was the next step. The first was getting someone in authority to hear him, to see that he was the wrong man, not this Dalton for whom he was being mistaken.

He had to risk it.

They were a dozen feet away when he shouted at them.

"Can't anyone around here see that I couldn't possibly be this Dalton character? For Christ's sake! Where the hell do you think I could have gotten these clothes? Chained to this fucking rock? Is everyone around here blind? Or just stupid?"

They turned, stared at him, then at each other. Christian could see the condescending amusement, tinged with sadism, that played about their faces. The smaller man spoke. With a mock salute, he said, "We'll be sure to give the commandant your message." Then they both laughed and walked away.

Christian watched them dwindle across the grassy expanse, still stunned at yet his second failure to achieve any kind of meaningful contact.

What was going on here? And what should I do?

The bucket of food—slop of some sort—sat in the dirt at his feet. He thought of the meals he had eaten without thinking about them all his life, and wondered if he would ever see another like them.

It was less than an hour later that three different soldiers returned. They stunned him by sauntering right into his circle, clutching him by his arms, and steering him toward the rock at the foot of his chain. Ignoring his now frantic protests, they bent him forward on his face and chest on the rock, spread his arms to either side of the boulder, and secured his wrists around the far base of the stone. They did this so expertly that Christian realized that they had performed this rite on many occasions. Then, clutching his shirt at the back of the collar, one of the men ripped it dramatically from his back with one sudden gesture, exposing his skin. He turned the fabric about in his hands curiously before shrugging and tossing it aside.

Tethered helplessly on his chest against the rock, his knees genuflecting in the dirt at its base, Christian managed to turn his face sidewise and squeeze a glance at his captors over his shoulder, his face pressed roughly against stone. He was very close to panic now, and what he saw triggered his outburst.

One of the men was brandishing a whip—a cat-o'-nine tails—with an expression on his face too much like pleasure.

"What the Christ do you think you're doing?" There was no restraint left in Christian's voice now; the time for it had passed. His question was a shriek of horror—the bleat of the civilized man who has never seen or contemplated such an atrocity to another human being.

"What does it look like, Dalton?" The man was flexing his wrist, shaking the leather tendrils loose in the sand.

"I'm not Dalton, you asshole!"

"Of course not. You're the fucking Chancellor of the Exchequer, and this is all a horrible mistake!" The three of them roared with laughter.

"Are you three blind? What's the matter with everyone around here?" The man with the whip was settling his feet ominously.

"Shut up, Dalton. Just shut up. That's why we're here—to shut you up. You're not supposed to be heard from or noticed until your time is up. You know that. You knew what would happen."

The first lash sent an incomprehensible shock through Fletcher Christian IV's system. This was beyond nightmare. In a nightmare, you always woke up at this point. He was not waking up. This was really happening.

In rage and pain and fear, he screamed.

But there was no lessening of the rhythm which had been established. The white-hot lashes continued to brand his soft urban skin, lacerating it pitilessly.

His brain fogged with pain, he was unable to count the volume of strokes that fell on his back. But if he hadn't undergone a numbing blackout about the halfway point, he would have realized that he had been the recipient of one hundred of her majesty's lashes, dispensed at the sole discretion of the officer in charge of the compound, under whose charter he was to be wholly subservient for the duration of his stay on Norfolk. When informed of the prisoner's outrageous behavior, Major Joseph Anderson had, with a sentence fragment and a dismissing wave of his hand, authorized the punishment. He had then passed his cup across the breakfast table to his wife, who had poured him a second cup of hot tea.

At either end of the table sat his two teenage daughters, Rebecca and Anne, listening with different degrees of curiosity and interest to the tales the guards had brought back with them from the prisoner's isolation circle. Rebecca, in particular, listened wide-eyed and alertly, and thought about the man in the chain a great deal as she buttered her bread and sipped her tea that morning.

*   *   *   *   *

Christian lay at the foot of the rock for several hours in an undulating state of consciousness and unconsciousness. It was, by his reckoning of the sun, well past noon before he attempted to push himself to his hands and knees, and then by degrees to his feet.

He knew without looking or touching what his back must be like. He knew that the tissue had opened to the bone in some places, and that in others it would never heal properly. He knew, too, that he would undoubtedly survive; floggings were not regarded as fatal punishment from everything he understood of the historical practice. But he also had new understanding of the term "scarred for life." If corporal punishment existed as a sanctioned legal activity in the twenty-first century, he was unaware of it. It was a matter of extreme insight to him just how close his modern and civilized world was to an age of utter barbarism.

He had never known such continuous pain in his life. His was an age when pain could be stifled or abbreviated; nothing in his experience matched the relentless aching and searing that the exposed nerve endings of the open flesh on his back were transmitting to his brain. And there would be no balm. He understood that. He would have to bear it. Somehow.

Later in the day, when no one had approached him in any way, he surrendered to the hunger that had been growing steadily since dawn. He approached the bucket that had been left that morning.

It was covered with flies. They were everywhere about the lip of the pail, buzzing and feeding, and a cursory glance within it revealed them in unsavory clusters there as well. This, combined with the now-rancid smell of whatever the food had once been, quelled Christian's hunger for the time being.

He left the bucket and returned to the rock—the scene of his recent incredible ordeal.

He thought. And waited. And tried to understand.

* * * * *

Night had fallen. And still no one had come near him. In the gathering darkness, he lay propped against the great rock at his side, the cooling air of the evening licking at his wounds. The scientist and scholar in him tried to grasp his milieu, the better to facilitate a plan, a path of any kind.

He knew that the spectacle of physical punishment as a legal process had virtually disappeared in the Western world by the beginning of the nineteenth century. The age of sobriety in public punishment had commenced. Paradoxically, it was England, he recalled, that was one of the countries most loath to dispense with it. She had no doubt feared the loss of power that it might signal during the social disturbances that were rampant everywhere at the onset of the 1800s.

He guessed, with accuracy, that he had experienced one of the vestiges of Empire, greedily maintained, its death throes twitching on the horizon.

He was on an English colony island, somewhere in the Pacific, he hazarded. Somewhere between 1750 and 1850 would be his next guess.

He mulled over his conclusions, the inferences of which had not yet taken clear shape for him.

And waited.

And tried to understand.

It was still dark. Christian estimated that it must be shortly before dawn. He had not slept at all that night in spite of his exhaustion.

A new theory had been evolving in his brain throughout the endless night, and he thought that he was on the right track. This didn't have to be a military prison compound; it might be a civil prison—one of the exiles designated by Britain as a place of transportation for criminals. Everyone knew the checkered history of Australia's settlement as a penal colony. Unfortunately, he didn't know enough specific history to tell him exactly where such colonies may have been in or around Australia.

He had thought that this was an island, but he could be wrong; it could be mainland Australia, near the coastline.

He remembered something about Tasmania and its early usage by Britain. What had it been called originally? Van Diemen's Land. That was it. Yes. And Sydney, too. It had originally been called Botany Bay, hadn't it? Another major penal settlement. Western Australia? That had been during the latter half of the nineteenth century, he seemed to recall, but couldn't be sure.

Perhaps this is Van Diemen's Land, he thought.

But why am I here? What happened?

He thought of Liana, and had to consciously will the ache that began in his chest to stop before it overwhelmed him. The Incan adventure had turned sour. If he was truly in the past, then none of what had happened to him had even happened yet. Including Liana. His life existed only within his head. Everything that he knew or had experienced had no objective correlative. His life was the future, but there was no future yet. And he wasn't even sure that there was any guarantee that there would be a future.

His thinking waffled between lucid, crisp metaphysical insights, and the total uncertainty of the mentality that slowly subsumes the imprisoned.

He contemplated his imprisonment. If this was indeed the nineteenth century, then it was the Classical age that had discovered the body as object and target of power. It meshed with his flogging, he realized, trying to establish a type of clinical detachment. Frederick II, Descartes, Man-the-Machine: a materialist reduction of human beings. Man could be controlled. He was a series of pulleys and wires. From Jean-Baptiste de La Salle, to Leibniz, through Buffon, the beliefs were shaped for the era, until they flowered in the man who wished to organize such a world through a political awareness of such mechanical detail: Napoleon Bonaparte.

Even this form of enslavement and public punishment was consistent with the rule of lateral effects: that the penalty must have its most intense effects on those who have not committed the crime. Man, being manipulable, was totally susceptible to such example, and lasting impressions would result from something as concrete as the scars and welts on Christian's back. Such was the philosophy of the time, at the dawn of scientific inquiry.

The age of Humanism had not yet been born.

And Christian realized that he could become a pawn of such unenlightenment. In fact, he already was.

The sun was bleeding the morning sky a hue of orange. As it blended with the purple of the receding night, Christian was reminded of the bruises and wales that had altered a part of him beyond recognition. He gave thanks that his mind was still unaffected, that it could still afford him the luxury of contemplative reflection and speculation as a temporary escape from pain. But the pain was coming back and he began to shudder with the physical reaction.

Then he saw the woman. Or perhaps she was merely a girl. She strolled a calculated distance away from him—some hundred meters or so—watching him with overt curiosity. She wore a long, blue dress.

For reasons that he didn't understand, she was the first person he had seen here that didn't fill him, at least in part, with fear. On the contrary. She gave him, on some level, hope, and he needed that. Perhaps it was the sudden intrusion of the feminine into the harsh masculine world.

He thought, again, of Liana.

When he stopped thinking of her, and concentrated on his present, he saw that the woman was heading away from him, heading toward the large mansion on the hill, perhaps a morning constitutional fulfilled. And he was alone again.

26

PITCAIRN ISLAND
1 July, 1972

Dalton studied the pretty, dark girl standing before him. She seemed to present no threat that he could determine. In fact, he was now realizing that she could prove very useful to him. She spoke English, but with an accent he did not recognize. And her features were definitely Polynesian, as was her skin coloring. There was something, though, about her features that he could not put his finger on—something that was not fully Indian; she was like a rare hybrid flower, raised in the heat and isolated care of an English greenhouse.

And they were alone.

Temptation for her loomed strongly in his brain and loins. But Dalton was not a blindly stupid man. Impulsive action would surely be his undoing. For a man who had endured prison, chains, flogging, and uncountable humiliations, patience and a type of fatal stoicism were the flowers that he had cultivated.

He would wait, and learn. And let the situation unfurl.

He glanced around, assuring himself that they were still alone. Again, he pulled his black hair away from his face and forehead, sweeping his large hands along his temples as he did so. His blue eyes dug deeply into the girl. "Is Pitcairn an English island?" he asked.

"Yes."

He cursed, silently.

"But that's a funny way of seeing it, I think."

He listened attentively.

"I mean, we're no more English than New Zealand or Australia. And a lot less so than either of them. We're ourselves. And we get the radio stations from Los Angeles as well as from anywhere. Their stations play the best music."

Some of the pieces were beginning to elude him. "Los Angeles," he said. "Where's that?"

She grinned a silly grin, looking at him curiously. Then, seeing that he did not appear to be fooling, and remembering his overall sense of confusion, she answered, "In California, of course." Then she added, uncertainly, "America."

America he had heard of often enough. He nodded, as though he understood.

"You're not an American, are you?" she asked.

"No."

She waited for him to elaborate, but he did not.

"What's a radio station?" he asked.

She wrinkled her nose and smiled. It was some kind of a joke, she knew.

But there was no humor in his face. His blue eyes were open and searching. Now it was her turn to look confused. "What do you mean, what's a radio station?"

"Is it a military post?"

"A radio station?"

"Who's stationed there?"

"Nobody's stationed there. It's where they broadcast the news from. And where they play the music from." She frowned. "Are you alright?"

He was quiet for a moment. "I don't know."

"Where are you from?"

He looked at the girl. "I'm lost."

She didn't know what he meant. But she did know that she believed him. He was lost. She could sense that. Maybe he'd lost his memory, she thought—been in an accident, a blow to the head perhaps. She'd heard of such things.

"You say your name is Lisa?"

She smiled and nodded.

"Well, Lisa," he said, "I'm going to need some help. A lot of help. And I'm going to need you to keep me a secret. Can you do that?"

Her heart raced. It was what she wanted, for now: an adventure, a secret, a—dare she hope it?—romance.

"Yes," she said. And she infused the word with a life of its own. "I'll help."

Dalton felt some of the fear and anxiety drain out of him. "Good," he said. "Thank you."

For a brief moment, he allowed himself a luxury he had been denied for too long. For just a moment, a fleeting instant, he entertained a vision of the future that did not contain pain or imprisonment. He let himself feel, briefly, a spark of hope.

27

NORFOLK ISLAND
3 July, 1835

Rebecca Anderson's interest in the prisoner chained to the rock was something that wasn't even clear to her. True, Dalton was the most notorious case of granite-like intransigence on the island, and as such presented her father with his most overt and direct challenge. In this sense, he had a much higher profile than other prisoners. His name had been mentioned more than once by her father at the dinner table. Her father, she knew, wanted to break him, to set an example for the others that would enter the mythology of the prisoners. He was convinced that this would provide him with a landmark victory in what he perceived as his private war against even the most remote possibility of seditious thinking.

Yet Rebecca couldn't hold to the vision of Dalton as enemy. Her opinion had taken rough shape that day back in March when the guards had escorted Dalton into her father's office. She had seen him being led in, and had been transfixed by the blood welling out of the side of his head and congealing on his neck and shirt. Instead of continuing on her way, she had hesitated, curious, and remained just outside the office door, out of sight but not out of earshot. She had listened to her father's ire foment and knew from her own experience that this Dalton stood no chance in its path. Even her mother knew better than to tread into his line when he had begun to boil. A part of her, right then, had felt some measure of pity for the man who stood powerless before him. No one crossed her father. Especially a prisoner. It could not be done.

But this man had stood his ground. Rebecca could scarcely believe what she was hearing. And she would never forget it. "I did nothing to merit this."

The prisoner's words still whispered to her from the recesses of her memory. It was incredible. The conviction of the tone, the simplicity of the statement—these things led Rebecca to believe that there was more than a strong possibility that the sentiment was true. How many times had she felt the same thing? But her father, she knew, would not respond to such a view; he never had, in her memory. His position had forged the outline of his personality, hammering it into what she thought of as the purest steel.

Dalton had stood no chance. None. And he must have known that.

Yet he had not backed down.

"I did nothing to merit this."

Rebecca had been fascinated.

From that point on, Dalton's circle had been a part of many of her itineraries. It was a form of voyeurism, at its simplest level; but at a more complex level, it was a tacit form of admiration. He became both man and symbol for her.

There was strange chemistry at work when she viewed him, chained and immobile, yet somehow capable of retaining dignity in the face of pain and deprivation.

And now there was something different.

It buzzed about in her brain like a housefly, landing and taking off, summoning an urge to swat it away.

But it would not go.

Something different

She continued her sewing. The words were still there.

"*I did nothing to merit this.*"

She finished breakfast quickly. "I'm going out, Momma."

"Oh. Where?"

"Just out."

Her mother shrugged. Rebecca's moods were nothing new. "Be home soon. I need your help."

"I will." She headed for the door.

What, her mother wondered again, does she find to do with herself? They had been posted to some desolate places, but Norfolk was by far the worst. And for a girl Rebecca's age? She could only shake her head at the thought of enduring such social isolation at such a tender crossroad. The girls should be thinking about marriage, family. And who, in God's name, were they ever going to meet here? One of the sentries? She shuddered. Joseph had promised that he would insist on a maximum three-year stay here, and then exact his privilege of requesting retirement in England. This sustained her. There was a limit to what was reasonable to ask of a family. There were the girls to consider, not just his career. She frowned at the memory of their habitual dialogues on the matter.

If he doesn't return to England within his three-year span, then we'll just have to go without him.

Enough is enough.

She wrung her hands.

Rebecca *knew* there was something fundamentally different about the man—different from what she had seen previously as well as different from everyone else on the island. Even as she stared at him, she sensed something missing from her perception, some link that had been dropped in her memory. It was puzzling, but did not obsess her.

He was staring at her—a shadow blowing by in a wind: something unreal, untouchable, mysterious. She did not belong here amid the ugliness and the brutality and the irrational contempt for life that hovered everywhere.

Like a flower in a storm.

Her hair was soft blonde, her face talcum smooth, her eyes a source of civilized haven.

And the blue dress. Unchanging. The same one he had come to identify her with. It fit her mien with poetic aptness—bright optimism like the clear sky of morning.

In a gesture of pure brass, a signal of rebellion more overt than any she had ever dared, she spoke to him.

"Hello."

The man who had been watching her with fascination looked positively stunned. But his amazement was colored with a flash of joy and hope that radiated like a star that seems to grow in luminescence in the night sky, then shimmer back to its normal glow Rebecca was quick to note its flare-up, alert to its waning. Nevertheless, the man looked wary. He glanced about to see if they were being observed or if anyone was within hearing distance.

No one was.

This was his chance. His first break.

He answered quietly. "Hello."

She greeted the word with a cautious smile.

Christian held his breath. He glanced around again to see if there was any danger in carrying on the exchange. None was apparent.

"Nobody's supposed to talk to you. And you're not supposed to talk to anybody either."

He nodded. "I know"

She stood about ten feet outside the radius of the circle that dictated his limit. "I'm Rebecca."

Christian was sitting with his legs crossed, feeling filthy and unpresentable suddenly. He became aware of the stubble on his face, the grime everywhere, the caked blood on his back.

But the morning was bright.

"I'm Fletcher Christian IV. Please call me Fletcher."

The girl looked puzzled. "You're Dalton. Everyone knows that."

He licked his lips. This was the point where he seemed to stumble in his previous attempts. His heart sped up as the crisis point culminated. His denial that he was Dalton seemed to provoke all the wrong responses in others.

"Please," he said, softly, "listen to me. I know this sounds crazy. I don't understand all of it myself. But it's true. I'm *not* Dalton. There's been a switch somehow." He tried not to convey the desperation that he felt. "Do I look like this Dalton? Is that why everyone keeps mistaking me for him?"

The sensation that resembled the housefly buzzing in her brain returned for an instant. *Something different.* Then it was gone, as quickly and as suddenly as it had appeared.

"How could you be anyone but Dalton?" She almost giggled. "What a fantastic story." Her tongue clucked in disapproval. "They say you've gone mad." She waited, her eyes twinkling.

He smiled wryly. "Sometimes I think I've gone mad, too."

She walked slowly to her left and seated herself gracefully on a large rock. He followed her with careful eyes, watching her fold her hands in her lap and continue to wait for him to tell her more.

He remained sitting in the sand, feeling the reminder of his steel confinement around his waist—the most incredible and frightening weight he had ever felt. Its presence tempered his words, made him choose what to say with the discretion of a man trapped who senses his best—and perhaps only—opportunity presenting itself to him.

"I'm not mad, Rebecca. In fact, I'm very sane. And I am definitely not this Dalton character."

She stared at him with the same disbelieving smile. Then she rose, as if to leave.

"Don't go."

She looked at him.

"Please."

"I'll get in trouble. You'll get in trouble." But she did not move.

He dropped his eyes, thinking. "You're right, of course. I don't want you to get in any trouble. But I'm already in trouble, so don't worry about me."

"It could be worse for you."

"How?" There was a long pause.

"I don't know. I don't know what Father might do. But he'd do something. I know that."

"Who is your father?"

"You don't know?" She watched him carefully.

He shook his head.

She continued to watch him, uncertain. It was true. He didn't seem to know who she was. She could read it in his face. "Major Anderson."

She detected no reaction, which puzzled her more.

"Who's Major Anderson?"

"I don't understand you," she said. She started to go.

"Please."

She stopped. "I can't stay."

"Come back then." He paused. "When you can."

She said nothing.

"Please."

She left.

He saw her coming in the last shafts of sunlight. It was after dinner. He had eaten as much of the gruel from the bucket as he could keep down.

Another chance.

He strove for the same calm that had worked so well for him that morning.

She sat on the rock. They both glanced about to ensure that they were not being noticed.

"Hello," he said.

"Hello."

His heart was racing.

"I can't stay long."

"I understand."

"Well, I don't."

He frowned.

"I don't understand why you're chained up like this. You don't seem like such a savage to me."

"Who says I'm a savage?"

"Everybody. My father."

"Ah, yes. Major Anderson." He nodded as if he understood. But he knew that he had to ask the questions that might confirm his madness in her eyes. He looked straight at her. "Why do they think I'm a savage?"

"It's just their way of saying that they can't control you. You defy them. And you talk back."

"This makes me a savage?"

She smiled. "You forget where you are."

"Yes," he said. "I do. Where am I?"

She wrinkled her face. "What?"

"Where am I? What's this place called?"

"You know where you are."

"But I don't. That's what I've been trying to tell everyone, but no one wants to listen. I'm not Dalton. I don't know where I am."

"I think you are crazy."

"Please," he said. "Humor me. Tell me where I am. Where we are. I really don't know."

She continued to gaze at him.

He stared into her eyes, trying to convey sincerity without words. Then he tried another tack. "Pretend I'm a victim of amnesia."

"What's that?"

"Loss of memory. No recollection of the past."

"Is it true? Is that what's happened to you?"

"No. But if we pretend, we'll be a lot closer to the truth than by assuming that I do know where I am and what's going on."

She thought about it. It seemed harmless. And if he was a savage, as everyone claimed, then he was an intelligent one. *Amnesia.* She'd have to look it up in the big dictionary. "You're on Norfolk Island."

Fletcher Christian IV let the place name sink into his brain. He had heard of it. He knew it well. His ancestors on Pitcairn had attempted settlement on Norfolk on two different occasions.

He knew, too, the rest of its history, and finally understood.

His fears were well-founded.

"Norfolk." The word dripped from his lips, hung in the air somberly, then evaporated into the evening breezes that whispered out of the tall pines.

She was waiting for him to continue.

His mind was spinning, and he had to will it to stop. "Norfolk." He repeated it once more, as much in shock as disbelief. "What year?"

"Pardon?"

He swallowed, licked his lips. "What year is this?"

"What year do you think it is? You haven't been here long enough to lose track of the years." She smiled with more than skepticism now. "But I forgot. It's like you have *amnesia,* right?" She was pleased to be able to use the strange word.

"Yes."

"1835."

He put his hand to his forehead and rubbed his temples. There seemed nothing to say. It merely confirmed what he had begun to deduce.

But he had hoped that he was wrong. He had clung to the chance that this was some sort of delusion, some sort of fluke that could be righted simply.

Now he knew that this was not the case.

1835.

What had happened to 1972? To Pitcairn?

Jesus Christ! Hold onto it, Christian. Don't lose it now! He fought back the first wave of pure panic, quelled it, and the ensuing waves diminished until he could once again cope.

"I should go," she said.

"And Major Anderson?" he asked. "He's the officer in charge of the island? Of the...prisoners?"

"Yes."

He nodded, the pieces sliding into place in his brain.

"I have to go."

He sat there, unmoving.

This time, though, she was the one who suggested it. "I'll come back."

Then she was gone.

He saw no one except his gaolers, his tormentors, for the next two days. In spite of this, he surprised himself with his patience. The days slid by uneventfully, lazily; long mornings, with drops of water on the ground that evaporated as the shadows shrank; endless afternoons, the air shimmering with heavy heat, followed by cooling evenings when the winds died down and the trees became still—punctuated only by the daily appearance of the slop bucket that was supposed to sustain him... He saw each day without interacting with it. He had ceased to exist without such interaction, and he began to understand the notion of isolation as he had not previously grasped it. Where such isolation led eventually, he could only speculate, but his imagination was fertile; he was capable of envisioning the loss of identity, the loss of esteem, the death of the ego. It was just a matter of time.

Until your existence stopped mattering.

Even to you.

The nights were the worst.

Christian sensed the flap at the corner of his mind that needed only to be peeled back to reveal the chasm of madness that would embrace the night's cold darkness. Sleep could be the only escape.

But even sleep failed.

For there were dreams, dreams such as he had never experienced nor had ever imagined he could experience.

Bombs, floggings, tall ships, entrapment, his parents, Liana, school days, meteorites, the university, Rebecca, the elongated tunnel between the centuries, women's breasts, thighs...

Each night he had awoken, sweating and shaking, at the moment of climax during a nocturnal emission, his seed and manhood erupting from him in a paroxysm of released tension.

His only escape.

And then he would lie there, the sweat turning cold, chilling him—wait until the morning.

Wait for her.

It was after he awoke the second night that he got the idea. It wasn't much of an idea, but it was something. It was worth a try.

He crawled from the scooped hollow in the earth and retrieved it from the base of the rock on which he had been strapped while being flogged—where it had fallen since being torn from his back by the guard. Then he crawled back into his hole, clutched it to his chest, and tried to formulate what he would say, how he would present it.

And waited for her.

And shook from something beyond cold, his teeth chattering, his brain reeling.

Morning. He waited for morning.

It seemed like forever.

She came.

He could only guess the time: probably nine or ten in the morning. An after-breakfast walk, he assumed.

He had been staring for hours without realizing it at the big house on the hill from which she would emerge. Only when she was more than two-thirds of the way toward him did it strike him what he was seeing, so hypnotic had his state become.

Her blue dress. Her blonde hair.

It was like waking up all over again.

He sat up, steadying himself

She meandered toward his circle slowly, circuitously. Her path took her ever closer, all the while trying to appear to a casual onlooker to be a random route.

Fletcher clutched the remnant of torn shirt in his hands. He had been clutching it maniacally since the middle of the night, since he had thought of it.

She came closer, from along the edge of the tree-line, through the tall grass.

He sat very still.

And finally, she sat on the rock, her rock, and spoke to him, her voice a musical note to his ears.

"Good morning."

"Good morning, Rebecca."

She smiled, and actually seemed to blush slightly at his familiarity. It seemed dangerous to her to cross this line, to use names. Perhaps it was this sense of danger that prompted her to respond with a smile instead of a rebuke: for it was comfortable danger—this man shackled as he was. The real danger lay in having her father learn of her visits. But this was something that she did not wish to think about; if she thought about it at length, she knew she would not have the courage to continue. As it was, she had suffered a two-day lapse of nerve during which she had second-guessed herself. It was boredom, though, that brought her back. *Ennui,* she reflected, enjoying another exotic word that she had only recently learned.

"What do you think about here?" she asked. "I get bored up at the house."

"It goes beyond boredom here, Rebecca." His voice was soft, comforting to her. "But I understand. I get bored."

"When did you lose your memory?"

"Pardon?"

"Was it before or after they chained you here the last time? I mean, what's the last thing you can remember?"

"The last thing I want to remember is talking to you. There's nothing I want to remember after that."

She blushed again. But she could see the possible motives beneath such apparent compliments, and was not as beguiled as she might have been. Still, it was nice to hear such things. She had heard them nowhere else since arriving.

"Your amnesia. When did it start?"

"I don't really have amnesia."

"But I thought you said you did."

"That would be dishonest. No, I said that it would be useful to pretend that I had amnesia, because I really do not belong here. I have been placed here mistakenly. I have been switched with this Dalton. He is gone. I am here now. You have to help me."

She stared at him for several seconds. "This is absurd."

"I can see how it would seem so."

"How can I accept such a fantastic story? Why do you tell such a story?"

"I tell it because it is true."

She was quiet for a bit.

"I'd like you to look at something."

"What?"

He held the torn shirt out to her, slowly, and with no possibility of interpreting it as a threat.

"That? Your shirt?"

He nodded.

"But why?"

"You'll understand better after you examine it." He continued to hold it in his hands as an offering.

"Tell me now why I should want to look at your shirt."

"Because it will tell you that I am unusual to possess such a shirt. Because it will intrigue you."

They stared at each other.

"May I?" he asked.

"May you what?"

"Give it to you?"

She chuckled, not without some nervousness. "You just want to get close enough to grab me. I'm not that foolish, you know."

"No," he said. "No. That's not it." He was afraid he would lose her if she thought anything like that. "You don't have to come within my reach. I'll toss it out to you. Really."

She measured the distance between them carefully with her eyes. He was about twenty feet inside his circle, she about fifteen feet outside it. If she remained where she was seated, he could not reach her. Was there something inside the shirt? A stone perhaps? The idea frightened her, but she was thankful that it had occurred to her.

"I want to see what's inside the shirt."

"What do you mean?"

"Unfold it. Shake it out." She held her breath. If her worst fears proved correct, then she would have been wrong about this man, and he would be shown to be the savage that others thought him. And she did not want to be wrong.

He did it. He unfolded it and held it up for her to view. It was torn down the front, and most of the buttons were missing. Otherwise, it was just a shirt. There had been nothing hidden in it.

She was glad.

Even at this distance, though, the shirt perplexed her. She realized she had never seen one like it. It was a muted gray, with a pattern of soft, white, thread-like lines crossing through it, creating an effect of squares. But was it cotton? She couldn't tell at that distance. Seemed much too light to be wool.

"All right." Her curiosity had gotten the better of her. "Toss it to me."

She sat nervously as the man rose, unsteadily, walked to the edge of his circle, the great chain clinking behind him as its length unfolded; he rolled the shirt up into a small ball and tossed it in her direction.

It landed at her feet. She glanced down as it opened like a living thing, settling itself comfortably.

Then she stared at the man. It was the closest she had been to him, the best chance she had had to see his features. She saw nothing of the savage in him. He was a man more than twice her age, she guessed, who radiated an aura of civilization, of intelligence.

It did not fit. Something was not right.

She looked back down at the shirt, dropping her eyes from him.

He watched as she bent and picked it up. She looked nervous.

Her hands touched the unknown fabric, sliding along its alien texture. It seemed wondrous, smooth beyond belief. Her skin prickled.

The fly buzzed in her brain again, disappeared.

"I have to go."

"Take it with you."

She nodded.

"Examine it. Please. Then come back and tell me what you think."

Her fingers stroked the shirt.

"Soon."

"Yes."

He watched her leave, a moth dwindling into the morning haze.

* * 28 * *

PITCAIRN ISLAND

3 July, 1972

Bran Michael Dalton waded out of the surf, his skin tingling with new zest, the sun heating the salty drops that sluiced down his body and dripped from his hair. Naked, he walked up the hill through the long grasses toward the cave where Lisa had taken him two days ago.

He shook his head, letting the water fly from his long hair, an animal movement he enjoyed. Then he grinned at the sheer physical satisfaction of it all. It had been a long time since he had felt such simple pleasure. Too long.

And such freedom.

He was alone. Lisa had not been around since the previous evening.

The three-minute walk was enough to dry him in the tropical sun, and when he reached the cave he plucked his pants off the bushes where they had been drying in the morning sun.

He looked up at the position of the sun in the sky. About eleven o'clock, he estimated.

The pants were dry. He pulled them on, buttoning them at the crotch and waist. As he did so, his eyes caught some of the debris at the mouth of his cave—debris that was his own—and he was once again snared in his own addled comprehension of what had happened and where he was.

But it was more than that. There were things that he simply didn't grasp—things that were not a part of the world he knew

Things that disoriented him totally.

He was looking at the metal containers that had held the food Lisa had brought him—empty now, piled at the side of the cave's mouth. Tins, she had called them. Tins of food. To be opened with that can-opener thing. It was astounding. There had been green beans in water inside one, with a picture of the vegetable on the exterior of the container. Another had baby carrots inside. Yet another had contained an assortment of fruit, all tasty and very sweet. And they all had the remarkable drawings of their contents on the exterior of each.

And a bar of soap that had lathered miraculously, and something called a sleeping bag, soft and downy, with the incredible zipper-thing running its length, and the finely detailed eating utensils... There had been so much that he had never seen before, never even knew existed... His problem was that he still didn't think a lot of it existed. At least, not in the world he knew. And that was why he still felt that he wasn't in any world that he knew. He was somewhere else.

But where?

He turned warily at the sound of someone walking along the path toward the cave and backed out of sight into the foliage.

It was Lisa.

He stepped forward, grateful to see her. She smiled the South Seas smile that warmed him like the trade winds, and he smiled back, drinking in the sight of her. As yet, he had not touched her. There was too much at stake, too much he did not understand, too much that he needed her for to risk it all for such a brazen urge.

But he wondered how much longer he could refrain. Her eyes, dark and playful, watched him.

"I brought you some more things." She shrugged a large pack from her back, caught it at her elbows, then eased it to the ground.

The movement arched her breasts against the bright red top she wore. Her arms, long and brown, were bare. His eyes were drawn to the long tanned legs that flashed from the shortened pants she wore – pants, he well-noted, that came only to her thighs. Her feet were bare as well. In all, she presented a heady package—a Polynesian sylph—to his Irish sensibilities, nurtured as they were in fogs and rains and woolen sweaters. What Dublin girls he could remember, like his own sweet Mary, were creatures of cloud and smoke and dampness; Lisa was sun and flowers and blue water.

In fact, the very idea of sex frightened him, and this as much as anything held him in check when he viewed her. Sex in Dublin had been of two sorts only: the whores along the quays of the Liffey, or coupling with a girl you might marry—like Mary Mullan. And the latter meant awesome responsibility; the kind of responsibility that his Da had borne so well but that he himself was not sure he could bear. It meant marriage and babies—always babies. There were eight in his own family. Bran had been the seventh. Only his sister, Jenny, was younger, and Mother had died giving birth to her. His Da had raised them though. His Da had been everything to Bran.

He had let him down. The look on his Da's face when the transportation to Norfolk had been pronounced was that of a broken man. Bran still saw the ashen face in his dreams, felt the palpable waves of pain that had issued from his father's eyes as they had led him from the dock that day.

Da...

Lisa was undoing buckles on the pack at her feet, jet hair trailing along her smooth, rounded shoulders.

"Some more tins of food..." She was reaching inside now

Her beauty evoked long-buried memories of his dark and tentative sexual encounters, few as they were. He had visited the whores on the quays a handful of times, each time suffering as much guilt as pleasure.

There had been one, though, sandy-haired Maag, whom he had sought more often than the others, because she seemed less-hardened, more vulnerable. Kinder.

Then there was Mary. He had never penetrated Mary. Never dared to. She had been special. They had been afraid of pregnancy and the shame it would heap upon her if she was not yet wed. And he had planned on wedding her—someday.

Now, he knew, she would take another as a husband, if she hadn't already. Nor could he blame her. She would never bear his sons and daughters, but another's. It was another of the many ways that he had ruined his life.

He thought of Maag and their furtive couplings, of Mary and their climactic fumblings, of the pleasure of their bodies, the frenzy of his need… He thought all this in an instant as he gazed down at the poetry of Lisa's feminine rhythms and lines, here, in this place called Pitcairn, which seemed unlike anywhere else on earth.

"And a radio." She pulled a rectangular cube from the pack at her feet and held it out to Bran. He took it from her, perplexed.

It was about the size of a brick, but made of some shiny, black material that he was unfamiliar with. It had small knobs, like the pulls on a chest of drawers, and a series of numbers were imprinted on a strip of glass along its top edge.

"What is it?" he asked.

"A radio!"

He held it at arm's length, letting the alien feel of it travel from his hands to his brain, but with no synthesis. "What do you do with it?" He tried pulling on one of the knobs to see if it would open. It seemed stuck, and he did not want to force it.

"What do you mean, what do you do with it? You listen to it, silly!"

He stared at it for a few seconds more, then lifted the thing to his right ear and listened.

Lisa's eyes widened in amazement. She watched him carefully for the next ten seconds. "You really don't know, do you?"

He looked at her.

"What to do with it, I mean."

He lowered the thing from his ear, shook his head slowly.

"You've never seen a radio?"

He shook his head again.

"I don't understand."

"You mentioned something called a radio station when we met."

"Yes."

"Is this a radio station?"

"No. The radio station is where they broadcast from. This is what you receive the broadcast on."

He held it curiously, weighing it, feeling its lightness. "What's it made of?"

"Plastic. The outside, anyway."

"What's plastic?"

"Bran... Her voice softened. "It's like you've been lost in the woods, or born and raised on a desert island, or something. These questions... 'What's a radio?...'"

He was quiet for a minute. "I don't know how to explain it."

She licked her lips. "Here. Let me show you." She took it from him. He watched as she extended two long, thin metal rods from each end of the cube, telescoping them to a length of more than two feet each. He hadn't realized that they were there. Then she turned one of the pulls and Bran jerked back at the sound that issued from the tiny device.

"Jesus, Mary and Joseph!" His eyes widened.

"It's the Stones. 'Satisfaction.'"

In shock and amazement, Bran Michael Dalton stared at the radio-thing, unable to close his mouth. His brain reeled at the cacophony of music and song howling from the tiny cube.

He glanced at Lisa. The sounds did not bother her. In fact, she seemed to be swaying, a slight smile on her face, listening intently to the vibrations and utterances.

His heart raced and his palms were damp.

Jesus help me! he thought. *What is that thing? Where am I?*

He had to stifle the urge to run, his insides twisting and knotting, his mind clinging to images of Lisa's face, the green lushness of the island, the white crests of the sea breaking below them—to things he could understand and find peace with while withstanding the assault of the unknown.

29

NORFOLK ISLAND
5 July, 1835

Alone in her room, Rebecca studied the shirt.

She had never seen anything like it. The seams were sewn so finely and invisibly that they were wondrous. The workmanship was beyond anything she had seen or anything she knew. And the fabric—so light, yet strong.

But it was the tiny tags sewn into the collar area that fascinated her the most; there were three of them. The topmost read: *65% Polyester 35% Cotton/Coton, Made in Malaysia.* Below that was a more prominent label: *Bahru Menswear, Singapore.* And finally, a tiny tag with numerals printed on it: *15 ½/33.*

Rebecca knew sewing: she prided herself on her familiarity with all aspects of the craft. But *this...*

She remembered his words. *Because it will tell you that I am unusual to possess such a shirt.*

Because it will intrigue you.

He had been right.

Harriet Anderson had watched from the second-storey window of their lushly appointed house as her daughter, Rebecca, walked away from the prisoner, to whom she had been talking.

It was not the first time. Harriet knew that. Her mother's instincts had alerted her to her daughter's swinging moods of late—moods more pronounced than what might be expected of a girl her age.

A *woman* her age, she amended.

She would speak to her. This could not continue. And if she persisted, she would have to tell Joseph. But that would be a last resort, for she harbored no illusions about the way he would take it.

He would be incensed. His *daughter!*

Harriet certainly did not wish that on their daughter. In fact, she seldom wished it on anyone.

She would speak to her. Tonight.

"Rebecca?"

She looked up from her sewing at the closed door of her room.

"Yes, Momma?"

"May I come in?"

"I'm decent."

The brass handle turned slowly on the door and her mother entered, carrying her own lamp. She set it on the oak chest of drawers just inside the door, where she could pick it up on her way out.

Rebecca was propped up in bed amid the softness of goose-feather pillows and eiderdown comforter. Norfolk's harshness did not extend inside the walls of the commandant's home. Her lamp glowed brightly on the bedside table. Rebecca let the hem of the dress she had been working on rest in her lap.

She smiled. "What is it, Momma?"

Harriet Anderson sat in the wingback chair to her daughter's left. Rebecca watched the finely lined face that had emerged over the years stare at her, saw her mother brush a strand of new gray over her ear with a casual movement of her hand.

"It has to stop."

Rebecca said nothing.

"There can be no more of it."

"What, Momma?"

"Visiting the prisoner. Dalton."

Rebecca bit her lip.

"Do you hear me?"

Rebecca nodded.

"Do you understand?"

"Yes." Her voice was a whisper.

"Your father doesn't know. Thank God."

Rebecca looked up at her mother. "You won't tell him? I mean, I might have to tell him. But if you tell him, the way you'd put it, it would be awful."

"What are you talking about? The way I'd put it? What does that mean? The whole thing is an enormous indiscretion, a monstrous error in judgement on your part, Rebecca. I thought you had better sense. What could come of it? At best, malicious gossip. At worst, undermining your own father and his position on the island." She omitted her actual worst fears, as an image of Rebecca and the prisoner writhing in sexual congress flashed from her subconscious, then receded back into the pool of outrageous and forbidden thoughts that she knew every decent Christian kept under control. Her sense of motherhood, too, was assaulted at the image, and her maternalism became forceful in spite of her vow to stay calm. "That's an end to it, understand?"

Rebecca was silent.

"Understand?" Her daughter's refusal to agree immediately sent a shudder of fear through her. This was an issue she wanted opened and closed as quickly as possible.

Rebecca seemed distracted, her mind inattentive.

"Answer me, young lady!"

"There's something strange about him, Momma."

"I don't care a whit if the man has two heads. You stay away from him, do you hear?"

"I hear you, Momma. Don't be angry with me. Please." She let a moment of conciliation settle between them. "But I still have to tell you about him."

"What in heaven's name could you have to tell me about a common criminal that would interest me or excuse your behavior? Honestly! Talk about addled adolescence…"

"He says he's not Dalton. He says there's been a mistake."

"And aren't you the perfect audience for his tales." Helpless scorn was creeping into her voice. This was not what she wanted, this confrontation with her daughter. She forced her hammering pulse to slow as best she could. Rebecca was a good girl, she reminded herself. That, she knew, was why she was so frightened. *What's gotten into her?*

"Momma?"

Harriet Anderson sighed heavily. "Yes?"

She pulled something out from under her pillow. "Look at this." She handed the shirt that had defied any known context to her mother.

"What is it?"

"Look at it. You tell me what it is."

She took the garment from her daughter's hand.

Rebecca watched the expression on her mother's face shift through a full range, like light filtering through a prism. Each nuance was a new shade of color and tone, soft shadows flickering in the room's lamplight. For more than a minute her mother examined the shirt, its mystery invading all her senses.

Finally, she spoke. "Where did you get this?"

"He gave it to me. It's his."

"What is it? Where did he get it?"

"I don't know. He hasn't told me yet."

"What do you mean, 'yet'? You're not going to see him again. I thought that was understood."

"But look at it! Can't you see—"

"I can see what I saw when I sat down here. I can see a young lady susceptible to tall tales and fancying a particularly unsavory human being, all of which disturbs me more than I can say! You're to stop this nonsense immediately!"

Rebecca watched the fire in her mother's eyes ignite in a way that was new to her.

"Rebecca?"

"Yes?"

"No more. Is that clear?"

Her heart sank. Without knowing it, she had just experienced her own version of the prisoner's inability to get anyone to heed truths which did not fit in with previously conceived notions. It was another door closing on the unknown, the obvious made impossible by fear. Harriet Anderson had plans for her daughters, and consorting with one of Norfolk's prisoners was not in the picture she projected. She refused to consider it.

At least overtly.

But what was the garment she held?

What was going on?

Rebecca made her own decision. It was a turning point in her life larger than she could know then, but she certainly sensed that it was leading away from the old life that she had always known and accepted.

"No more," her mother repeated.

"Alright, Momma," she said. But she knew she was lying. It was the only way she could see at that time.

30

PITCAIRN ISLAND
3 July, 1972

Lisa had left the radio on for about ten minutes, much to the bewilderment and consternation of Bran Michael Dalton, who sat alternately fixated on its mystery and then withdrawn into a secret place in his head, where he watched the scene as from a point atop a nearby palm tree.

When she finally turned the knob on the front and the thing fell silent, he experienced a wave of relief. The sounds of the birds and the wash of the sea were infinitely welcome, recognizable as they were. His senses literally buzzed as he oriented himself once more; in spite of the pleasant breezes, he was sweating.

Lisa had said nothing since the radio had begun to issue its unearthly music. And there had been another two songs, accompanied by instruments with which he had no familiarity, interspersed by the rapid chatter of a man's speaking voice. Most of what he said had been all but unintelligible to Dalton, but he was speaking English, and at one point Dalton caught the mention of Auckland.

"So, what do you think?" she asked. She seemed bemused at his wide-eyed silence.

"I don't know," he said. "Where do the sounds come from? Why are they in there?"

"They're not *in* there—at least, not the way you mean! That's a New Zealand station. We could listen to Tahiti, but that's French mostly. My father's radio, which is much better, can get Los Angeles, and other stations in the States. It's a beauty."

Dalton stared, some of what she was saying sinking in. He glanced at the radio, then back at her. Starting to speak, he hesitated, then tried again. "Those were voices in New Zealand?" Even as he asked it, it sounded ludicrous. And yet…

"Yes."

"How? How is it possible?" His voice rose on the last syllable.

"She looked at him with a mischievous smile, enjoying his bewilderment. It was not often that she was in a position of superiority to anyone in any way. To know things that another did not, no matter how elementary, was pleasant indeed.

"They're called radio waves," she said. "They travel through the air. These," she indicated the extended metal rods, "pick up the waves and broadcast them through the speaker." She pointed at a perforated area in the plastic covering of the radio.

"Where are these waves?"

Her nose wrinkled. "You can't see them! They're invisible!"

Invisible waves… Voices from a box…

Ghosts…

A sorcerer's island…?

But the sun shining down was real. So was the earth on which he was sitting, and the salt ocean from which he had recently emerged.

And this girl.

Very real.

Without realizing it, he had been staring at her. Lisa, however, was quick to notice his attention. And his vulnerability. And his broad, matted chest; his dark eyes, like tunnels into the night.

She placed her hand on his forearm and he felt her touch like a brand, a shiver that ignited small fires through his whole body. A warm rain on a cool evening.

"Lisa." He said her name once, then she took the initiative, as she had sensed she would have to from the beginning, and touched him with her other hand on the side of his neck. Again, the contact seared him, and his blood quickened, responding without choice.

She kissed him.

His senses flooded under the warmth and softness of her mouth. He was entering a grotto of liquid twilight, a labyrinth of arcane and unimagined pleasures. Then the deprivation of his recent life gave way like a dam of sticks and mud in a torrent, and he felt his body slip through the break.

Her mouth opened to him. Shaking, he held her by her shoulders, then, tentatively dropped his hands to the fullness of her breasts.

Her hand trailed along his chest, touched his waist, and moved to his hardness.

His breathing was ragged, frantic. This was impossible, he thought. This beauty, this fragrant, heady mixture of all things feminine, of satin and oil—his, for the taking, here, now

He swept his hands under her red top, along her lean midriff, gathering her breasts, stroking them lovingly, feeling her nipples harden, his own aching stiffness threatening to drive him mad. Overcome, he dragged her shirt up to her neck and pressed himself against the length of her body.

"Lisa." The word was part prayer, part invocation. His mind swirled.

"Wait."

He heard, but could not wait.

"In the bag."

He angled himself over her.

She pulled his head to her face and whispered into his ear. "I have safes in the bag."

Dalton paid no attention to her words. His hands were fumbling at her shorts now, opening them, sliding along the plane of her flat, brown stomach…

Touching her.

His fingers probed her moistness.

She pushed the shorts the rest of the way down her legs and opened herself for him. The ache of the months of torment and denial had brought him to a point far beyond recall. With trembling hands he unbuttoned his pants, letting his strained erection fall into her hands, and he gasped audibly, then groaned and shuddered, all the while trying to cling to some vestige of control. He felt a wetness on his cheeks, and it occurred to him that he may be crying.

Their hands twisting, caressing, Lisa spoke again. "You have to wear a safe. They're in the bag."

Dalton did not acknowledge that he had heard.

"No. Stop."

This time the words registered. He shook himself free of his overpowering lust temporarily, staring at her with little comprehension. "What do you mean, 'Stop'?" His eyes were wild.

"Not stop forever," she said, stroking his face. "Just long enough to put on some protection." She glanced toward the bag. "Bring it here."

He rolled onto his side and looked at the sack. "What are you talking about?" He was not going to be denied now. She had started this. Did she think she could get a man aroused like this and then just casually stop? He was astounded.

"The bag. Hand it to me."

Without breaking contact with her flesh, Dalton leaned and pulled the bag toward them, bewildered. She smiled coyly and reached inside, pulling out a packet of three identical small squares, made of some material that he was, as had become the pattern, unfamiliar with. She tore one off and dropped the remaining two back into the bag and pushed it aside.

"Here," she said.

He took the smooth, slippery square packet from her. "What is it?"

She giggled.

Dalton was not amused, and it must have shown in his face, for the girl quickly let the silliness fade from her in response. "It's a safe."

Dalton, showing no sign of understanding, conveyed to her once more his ignorance of all the rudiments of her world. Although it continued to amaze her, she nevertheless was beginning to accept and react to his plight with less incredulity each time she encountered another example.

"Here," she said. Holding the packet by a corner, she tore it opened and extracted a round, almost transparent object. It glistened, sheened with something lubricious.

He took it in his fingers, rolling it softly, feeling its slippery texture, wondering what exactly it was for.

"Put it on."

He looked at her.

"Here." She pointed, touched.

His eyes widened.

"You don't want me to get pregnant, do you?"

The words themselves horrified him, taking him back to his Dublin memories, slightly sobering his lust.

Then he understood. He had heard of such things, but had never seen one. No one he knew had ever seen one. *A French letter.*

"I've never used one," he confessed.

"Here," she said, taking the initiative. Oblivious to his gasp, she placed the item on the crowning glory of his penis. Then she proceeded, to his wonder, to unroll the device down his shaft, enclosing him in a sensuous, slick, tight world, elasticized and protected.

He stared down at himself in awe.

"What do you think?" she asked.

"A sheep's stomach."

"Pardon?"

"A sheep's stomach. That's what they're made of. A sheep's stomach." She laughed.

"It's true. I've heard it from a doctor himself."

She kissed him. "Not this one, sweetie." She lay back, keeping him close, maneuvering him. "Rubber."

For the first time in their heated encounter, Bran smiled. "I'd love to rub her."

Lisa laughed aloud. But when his hand began to do what he had just said, she began to purr and let Bran Michael Dalton, the man from she knew not where, enter her. With a kind of ethereal madness singing in his brain, he exploded, purging his body of a lifetime of seminal aching, collapsing, drowning, in her warmth.

Afterward, she held him tightly, for a long time.

And he thought again, the thought that had slipped into his brain earlier, unbidden

A sorcerer's island...

IV

*The sole cause of man's unhappiness is that he does
not know how to stay quietly in his room.*

— Pascal

*All the stream that's roaring by
Came out of a needle's eye;
Things unborn, things that are gone,
From needle's eye still goad it on.*

— W. B. Yeats, "A Needle's Eye"

VI

* * 31 * *

LIMA, PERU
9 July, 2072

Like nearly everyone else on the planet, Alfred de Baudin had also watched the vidnetworks during the live transmissions from Cuzco. And like everyone else, he too had seen the stunned look of horror and heard the utterances of Huascar after Fletcher Christian IV had disappeared.

"I've lost him."

De Baudin had felt his scalp prickle.

"He's gone... Into Time."

It had been nine days ago, but de Baudin still felt the same sensation of chills and dread when he thought about it. It was what the world must have felt back in the 1980s, he thought, when the American space shuttle *Challenger* had exploded in front of the world's unbelieving eyes, or when Saleem Khan and his entire cabinet had been erased from the face of the earth by the firebombs in Kuwait in 2034. It happened. Every so often it happened. And the world watched, privy to horror, confidant to tragedy.

Christian was gone. The man he had interviewed less than a month ago at the Atahualpa Gallery, surrounded by the heritage of the Incas, had disappeared. Huascar had seen it from the moment it had happened— had known that Christian would not be returning. He had seen his own failure as a failure for the New Incas, with ramifications far beyond himself, and in that, de Baudin reflected, he had probably been right. Huascar had understood that the event could cripple the church—that it might be read by many in quite unflattering terms. And for these reasons, and for the purging of his own soul, Huascar had gone into seclusion to meditate.

"Something took him."

"Something awful."

The words had rung in his ears when he heard them, and still taunted him on a daily basis. Huascar had spoken little to the press or to the public since it happened, but he had mentioned the shape and image of the specter that had intruded on his temporal transmission, briefly and fumblingly. No one could misinterpret what he was describing.

A bomb. A nuclear explosion.

The mushroom cloud.

Nine days ago. And Christian should have returned two days ago, if he was coming back at all.

The world now believed. Fletcher Christian IV was not returning, and the world, like Huascar, had, for the most part, gone into seclusion to meditate.

What had happened?

De Baudin had an idea. Just an inkling.

He spent the rest of that day at his computer console, poring through the bytes of stored information that he summoned up from the central library.

July, 1972. The Bomb.

He cross-referenced.

*   *   *   *   *

In her hotel room in Cuzco, Liana Christian started as the vidphone beeped. The sound set her heart racing. News, she thought. There might be some news. She had assured herself that the press did not have access to this code, so whoever was on the other end of the line should be some-one with something of import to tell her.

Her hand darted to the audio button. "Yes?"

"Liana Christian, please."

"Speaking." She breathed deeply.

"It's Alfred de Baudin calling, Mrs. Christian. I interviewed your hus-band here in Lima back on June 14th, at the Atahualpa Gallery."

"I remember well, Mr. de Baudin. What can I do for you?"

"I have to speak to Huascar. And to you."

"Huascar is in seclusion. No one except his closest spiritual advisors are communicating with him."

"You have to get through to him."

"Why, Mr. de Baudin? What purpose can this serve at this time?"

"Getting through to you was almost impossible. I think getting through to Huascar is something only you can do. I have to talk to him. I have to talk to you. *We* have to talk to him."

"About what? You still haven't said."

"About your husband. About what happened to him. About why he hasn't returned. I think I may know."

Liana pressed the video button. The look of passion and anguish on Alfred de Baudin's face startled her.

"You know?" she asked. Her voice was low.

He nodded. "I think so."

She closed her eyes, feeling dizzy.

*   *   *   *   *

Ecuador.

The equator passed through Ecuador, and the Andean slopes soared toward the sun.

Huascar was as close to his gods as he could be here.

Ingapirca lay at an altitude of 3160 meters in a triangular level between two rivers: the Silante on the north and the Huayrapungo to the south. Built in 1497 by order of the Inca king Huayna-Capac, it was now ruins. And it had originally, no doubt, been built on the ruins of a ceremonial complex much older than the culture of the Incas, a culture that also paid homage to the great god that was the Sun.

This was Huascar's retreat.

It was not the first time that he had come here, or asked to be brought here, to commune in silence with the gods. Alone.

There was much to think about.

The sun shone brightly, but the air was blessedly cool. It was the third day of Huascar's three-day withdrawal. His search for guidance was nearing an end; his mind was clear.

Calm.

They would return for him at sunset. He hoped that he would have some insight by then, but he was beginning to doubt, to feel abandoned.

My power, he thought. O Sun! Why have you forsaken me? His startling blue eyes gazed unwaveringly upward into the blue, endless sky.

There were no clouds.

He walked to the east of the ruins, where there was a spring of crystal water. It had rained the night before—quick showers that disappeared across the mountain tops as quickly as they had come. Water still drained down the slopes. The spring pooled before it tumbled down the rocky steeps, and the ground around it steamed in the morning sun, creating small rainbows where the water had collected in stony crevices. With the sun on his back, Huascar contemplated the vision of shimmering vapors and tiny rainbows, knowing that the answer was here, somewhere, if he only had the wisdom to see it.

He gazed across at the range of mountains that stabbed the sky in the distance, magnificent in purple and white and all other hues of the sungod's palette.

Perhaps, reflected Huascar, this is the significance of Ingapirca, of this chosen site. Perhaps some ancient priest had seen the harmony of the mountain peaks, the waters, the sun's rainbows, and built the ceremonial complex in the midst of this ancient juncture. Perhaps he had stood here, fronting an assembly that had watched and understood the vapors rising from the ground, disappearing beyond the peaks that were venerated as the dwelling places of the gods, and had seen in the myriad of glorious, small rainbows the fusion of the powers that dominated their world: the communication of the sun with the universe.

And he was the vessel that sailed through the sea of light from the sun, through the rainbows, to unite the spiritual world with the physical.

This land that had seen glaciers slide through its corridors, sprung up hot springs in its sunken valleys, fossilized the bones of mastodon, horse, and camel, was singing to him of a truth he might never grasp.

He sat on a rock and let it flow over him.

And prayed that the nightmare that he had glimpsed on the *usno* would fade back to whatever hell it had risen from.

Huascar saw the truck approaching before he heard it. Even at sunset the air was bitingly clear, and he watched the snakelike trail that the truck wove as it ascended the narrow road from the valley's entrance.

It was early for its arrival, and he wondered at this.

As it drew nearer, he was able to make out the presence of two other people besides his driver. In calm mental straits, he pondered this.

It was a man and a woman. He recognized the woman as the vehicle closed the distance.

It was Liana Christian.

Huascar steeled his eyes, sensing a breakthrough. Something had happened, he thought. Why else would she be here?

He raised his eyes to the mountain tops across the valley.

The gods, he thought. They will ever surprise us.

* * * * *

Liana Christian and the male stranger walked across the dusty ground toward Huascar. He remained seated on the immense stone slab that he had occupied for the last few hours. His body, ancient as it was, was still capable of inuring itself to the pains and proclivities of lesser men; a testimony to the powers of his mind, the nature of his meditation. Proof to him that his gods cared.

Huascar bowed politely to them both.

For a moment, the three froze in the metaphysical tableau atop the Andean peak, enshrined by the sun sinking behind them, bathing everything in its warm, orange glow. A small breeze scuttled some dust, stirred the wrists and ankles of their garments, then died.

Huascar waited.

It was Liana who spoke. "We think we know what happened."

Huascar stared at her face. He saw the hope, the fear. "This man has a theory that is worth listening to." She indicated the stranger at her side.

Huascar turned his gaze upon the man. He apprised his modest stature, his graying hair. He noted, too, the intelligence in the man's eyes. Huascar let his own eyes probe and judge, as he always did, relying on his ability to sense beyond the senses, to see what others could not.

He saw the past and the future simultaneously in the man's eyes.

"This is Alfred de Baudin," said Liana.

Huascar broke his silence. "Sit down, please." He indicated the shattered stone pillars lying to his left.

Glancing at one another, they sat.

Huascar looked back at the man and felt a tingle. The gods, he thought. *They will ever surprise us.*

He recalled his initial visit from Alejandro, the Venezuelan pope, in his chambers in Cuzco, many years ago. He had appreciated the wisdom of the man in his willingness to consider that which had previously been untenable for him. It had impressed Huascar, this open-mindedness, because it spoke of the proper degree of humility when confronted with the unfathomable.

Everyone, he thought, has their turn come round.

"I will listen," he said.

It had taken many minutes to digest.

"It was the bomb, then," said Huascar.

"It fits," said de Baudin.

"Yes," said Huascar, thinking aloud. "It does." He fell silent.

"One hundred years ago, to the day," said de Baudin. "What else could it be?"

It needed no reply.

"The bomb disrupted the arc through time."

"And sent him where? When?" asked Huascar.

It was de Baudin's turn to fall silent. "We can't know. What kind of paths exist through time? What is the nature of the forces that are operating here? These things are unanswerable."

Liana grasped de Baudin's forearm, squeezing it fiercely. "Tell him the rest. Tell him what you think." Her face was drawn, tense.

They both looked at her.

De Baudin turned to face Huascar again. "If," he said, "the power of the bomb blast warped all the time lanes sufficiently to propel or draw him elsewhere in time and/or space, it might be reasonable to assume that a similar attempt at reverse transmission at a further hundred-year interval from another similar bomb blast in the same area may be able to draw him back. It would seem that you and your powers need the un-measurable interference of the split atom to effect any broaching of the rigid hundred-year trajectory that has worked so far. Did the blast launch him an immeasurable distance from his original destination? We can't know. But we can operate within certain logical assumptions, for want of any other direction. He may have been transported to some other loca-tion besides Pitcairn—some place that also has strong vibrations for his own personal and family background. Tahiti? Perhaps. The bomb blasts of the 1970s occurred at Mururoa Atoll, within a range of disturbance for most of the area of the South Pacific that could have been within the compass of Fletcher Christian's illustrious heritage." He paused. "These are my thoughts."

Huascar contemplated. Then: "Your conclusions have been general. Do you have a specific plan? A specific date for this next bomb test in the 1970s, when we might attempt to extract him from the past?"

De Baudin glanced at Liana almost remorsefully. She avoided his face. Then he spoke to Huascar. "The next atmospheric test in the area didn't occur until August 16, 1973."

Huascar said nothing, but he thought he understood.

"What I'm saying," de Baudin continued, "is that the soonest logical attempt to extract him from his time/space would be one hundred years from that date—just as the blast one hundred years from July 1 removed him from the time lanes in the first place."

"Over a year from now," commented Huascar.

De Baudin nodded.

"He would remain another year wherever and whenever he is."

De Baudin let Huascar settle his thoughts. It took a few moments.

Finally, Huascar turned his blue eyes on them, piercing them like steel shafts. "Everyone's life is a tragedy," he said. "It is only a matter of when."

32

SOUTH PACIFIC
12 August, 1972

It was winter in the South Pacific, and the rains came.

McTaggart's arms ached as he held fast to the tiller of the *Vega,* on the last leg of her journey between Rarotonga and New Zealand. He had flown from Rarotonga to Vancouver, where he had spent more than three weeks.

No one had paid him any serious attention, including Prime Minister Pierre Elliott Trudeau, with whom he had chanced to speak for some forty minutes on his yacht off the British Columbia coast.

McTaggart had no way of knowing then that Canada had been one of the major participants in a quiet gathering in Paris, in February, some six months earlier, to form a cartel arrangement for uranium prices, to divide up the global marketplace in such a way as to determine the base price, which they could subsequently control with an iron fist. He couldn't know that customs officials in New Zealand would seize his boat upon docking in Auckland, and would find yet another irregularity to flog him with legally; this time it would be the generator that had been donated for his craft: its lineage was highly questionable, having no proper papers *in patria.* He had no way of anticipating the attitude of the press in both

Australia and New Zealand, which closed its jaws on the whole anti-nuclear movement with a ferocity that belied any neutrality of vision.

He could see or know none of this. All he knew was that no one cared. He was more than a nuisance, more than an outcast. He was a global leper, dismissed by all.

So he had flown back to Rarotonga, back to the speck in the Pacific that harbored his boat, back to his mates, for the final segment of the cruise that had hooped the French islands these last months.

Back to New Zealand. Back to Ann-Marie...

Nigel was sick. Grant looked like a ghost. He hated to think what he himself must look like, because he knew how he felt. Abandoned. His soul charred.

He had been at the brink of nature's most unimaginable power, and had sensed how they were all mere dust motes in its wake.

He sailed on.

At his back, at his front, on every side, ghosts swirled like vast storm clouds, moving with hurricane grimness toward the crack that had surfaced in the rock of time.

V

you must say words, as long as there are any, until they find me, until they say me, strange pain, strange sin, you must go on, perhaps it's done already, perhaps they have said me already, perhaps they have carried me to the threshold of my story, before the door that opens on my story, that would surprise me, if it opens, it will be I, it will be the silence, where I am, I don't know, I'll never know, in the silence you don't know, you must go on, I can't go on, I'll go on.

— Samuel Beckett, *The Unnameable*

V

* * 33 * *

NORFOLK ISLAND
7 July, 1835

Harriet Anderson lay in bed beside the sleeping figure of her husband and listened to the stealthy sounds of her daughter, Rebecca, as she slipped down the stairs and out the front door. It was almost midnight. Why? she thought. Why is she doing this?

To stop her would be to risk waking Joseph. And then there would be the ensuing confrontation—something that was appalling merely to contemplate.

She lay as if paralyzed. Gone, she thought. To see that man again.

What should I do?

It was a parent's nightmare. How do you stop your child from making mistakes as they grow up? How do you stop them from growing up?

And Rebecca, especially. What had possessed her?

Harriet Anderson contemplated, in a fretful manner, all the incidents and dialogues that may have presaged this bit of rebellion on the part of her formerly submissive daughter.

Growing up was one thing. But this kind of outright change? It was eerie—truly frightening in its suddenness. Harriet was not prepared. Not at all.

She lay there, confronted with something quite beyond her limited scope as a mother.

If she's not back soon, I'll simply go and get her, she thought.

But the thought upset her more than she could have imagined. What would she find if she went there?

And why is she doing this?

She waited an interminable hour. Then, casually and silently, she slipped from the bed, standing a moment to ensure that her husband still slept.

The rhythms of his breathing remained unchanged.

Moving to the closet, she took down a dress, undergarments, and a sweater that buttoned down the front, all the while moving with a slowness that was almost an ache. It had to remain her secret, as long as possible. I'm her mother—a woman. I understand, as he cannot, she thought, glancing at the blanketed form of her husband.

With Joseph Anderson, discipline was the focus of life. The military, and his peculiar place in the military scheme of things, colored every aspect of his philosophy. She could live with that, as long as it affected them as a family only peripherally. But it was not the way she saw life—nor, she was now realizing, was it the way Rebecca saw it, either. Women and men, she reflected as she drew on her clothing. The spaces between us are vast.

She closed the door silently behind her, eased down the oak stairs and out the front door—the second time that night that an Anderson woman had performed such a delicate escape.

Escape. The word in her head caught her by surprise. Yes, she thought. We are all trying to escape. Here, on Norfolk. And everywhere.

In the moonlight, she followed her daughter's secret footsteps.

From where she stood, behind the cover of trees and darkness, Harriet Anderson could see them.

They were talking, conversing, like any two civilized people. That was all they were doing, and Harriet breathed a bone-deep sigh of relief. Her hands, she realized, had been shaking all the while. They shook now, but less so, now that she was aware of them.

Now that the worst had not happened.

Rebecca was seated on a rock, listening more than talking. And although the actual words could not be heard at this distance, the tones indicated patience and an open stream of communication, the ebb and flow that speaks of two people who are doing more than just talking to one another—but two people who are *enjoying* talking to one another.

She watched, remembering how it had once been like that between Joseph and herself, a long time ago.

She moved closer, feeling some shame at wanting to hear. But she could not help herself.

And the fear was still there. Only a touch, true. But there, nevertheless. The man was a criminal after all. This could lead to nothing good.

What had Rebecca said? *"He says he's not Dalton. He says there's been a mistake."*

And there was the shirt…

She crouched, straining, listening, until finally she could hear the words.

Until she was bewildered.

Fletcher Christian IV knew how fantastic it must all sound. But at some point, it had to be told. People had to believe. It was his only hope.

And this girl, this Rebecca, she was the gateway out of this circle of torment. He cast his lot with her.

"I'm from the future," he said.

She giggled softly. "That's absurd."

He smiled and bowed his head before looking back at her. "Yes. It is. Nevertheless, it's true."

"How far in the future?" she asked, playing his game.

"About two hundred and fifty years." Then he calculated mentally. "You say this is 1835?"

"Of course it is."

"Then it's two hundred and thirty-seven years in the future, to be exact. I'm from the year 2072."

"That's fantastic. You're being ridiculous!"

"It might be easier if it wasn't true. Easier on a lot of people." He thought of his future life, of Liana.

"How did you get here then?" Her tone still indicated that she considered their conversation a form of verbal sport.

He paused. "Partly by design. Partly by accident."

"I'd say it was an enormous accident, judging from your plight."

He glanced down and touched the chain. "Yes," he said. "I guess you're right."

"No one would come from the future and put themselves into prison on Norfolk Island. That's a little hard to swallow."

"It's all a little hard to swallow. I grant that."

"If I were going to visit the past, I'd pick some place grand and exciting—some place with some wonderful historic beauty or importance. Not Norfolk!" She made a play of shuddering. "Like Rome. Greece. Paris. Like that."

He nodded. "There are restrictions."

"I see. You can only visit penal colonies. The vilest places on earth." She smiled.

He smiled gently in response. Her tone and attitude only indicated her intelligence and common sense. The skepticism she displayed was healthy skepticism. The scientist in him could only admire it; the man, fearful and trying not to become desperate, was at its mercy.

"First," he continued, "we are limited to a certain geographical trajectory, and to certain geographical points in our heritage; second, we have not—until now—broken the temporal range of one hundred years. So I was attempting to travel back in time to Pitcairn Island, one hundred years in my past—the island of my direct ancestry. I sought Pitcairn in 1972; I achieved Norfolk in 1835. Also, I have apparently displaced another man—this Dalton. God knows where, or when, he is. This was the accident part. Nothing like this had ever happened before."

"Why did it happen? What would have gone wrong?"

He shook his head. "I'd just be guessing."

"Amuse me."

She was lovely. And for her beauty and her naiveté, his heart ached. Yet she listened, for whatever reasons, to his tale, while others shunned and beat him. She deserved whatever he could tell her. But how much could she absorb? How much would she absorb?

His own theory about what may have transpired was as insubstantial as the future he had left behind. Yet there was the lingering image of the mushroom cloud, the nightmare vision that he could not shake.

"Something interfered," he said. "Something very powerful."

She remained silent, waiting.

"I think it was a bomb, somewhere in the past, somewhere in the vicinity of my intended destination."

"You mean an explosion? Gunpowder?"

"Bigger. Much bigger. A nuclear explosion."

"I don't understand you."

"I know. Sometimes I don't understand myself."

"Yet I don't think you're a fool."

"Another debatable point."

"You're too intelligent."

He looked at her.

"I think," she said, "that you are here by some sort of mistake. You certainly aren't like the others. You're much more civilized than even the guards here. And you've had some sort of schooling—that's evident from your language. Can you read?"

He smiled. "Yes."

"There. You see! Where would a common criminal learn to read? You're from a family of some means, hiding your origins."

"Why would I do that?"

"To keep the shame of your crime from your family. Maybe you were related to the royal family." She smirked.

"What nationality was Dalton?"

She frowned, then remembered. "Irish."

"Does my accent sound Irish?"

The fly buzzed in her brain again. "No."

"Does it sound British?"

"No."

"What then?"

She was quiet for a moment, reflecting. Then she asked, "What nationality are you, then?"

"I'm a Canadian. Do you know Canada?"

"Upper Canada and Lower Canada, yes. The colonies. But then you're British—or French. That's it! Originally French, now fluent in English. That's your accent. The French influence is almost gone. Fascinating!"

"Don't you see, Rebecca? My accent, the shirt, my education—I can't be Dalton."

"Nevertheless, you were arrested in Dublin and convicted as Dalton. Perhaps you fled the colonies and assumed an alias. Were you wanted for crimes?"

Christian exhaled slowly, stifling exasperation. "I need to see your father."

"Impossible."

"Why?"

"My father is a busy man. He has no dealings with the prisoners. Not unless it's of a disciplinary nature. And I'm sure you wouldn't want that."

"I'm a special case. That's what I've been trying to get you to see."

"You're bright. And you're imaginative!"

"And I'm from the future."

"I'm tempted to just say 'rubbish' to that. But it's such an intriguing tale." In the moonlight, her eyes sparkled. "Tell me something about the future that will convince me that you're from there!" Her tone held mock challenge.

He paused. "Ask me something."

She pounced with her question. "Can we fly in the future? People dream about flying. I read about Daedalus and Icarus. And my father has some books by Cyrano de Bergerac. In one of them, people are carried to the moon on burning gases."

"You read a lot?"

"Yes. There isn't much else to do much of the time."

He mulled this over. Yes, he thought. I can see that. Servants to tend to the menial tasks. She would be privileged. "Who taught you to read?"

"We had our own tutors. Back in London. Father thought at the time that it was a waste, but he's glad now."

"Your father showed sound judgement. Your mind is too keen to lie dormant. Reading will open the world to you."

"You see," she said. "Prisoners don't think about reading, about books. You're different."

"I told you. I am different."

"You haven't answered me."

He nodded. "Yes. People can fly in the future."

"How?" she asked, challenging him further. "Balloons?"

"Yes. That's one way. There are also airplanes, rockets, gyros, gliders… People fly from country to country in great ships with wings—ships that hold hundreds of people. There are stations that orbit the earth—above the clouds—and people can commute to them by flying ships called space shuttles. Rockets can travel to other planets, to the moon." He had no idea whether she would believe him.

She barged on. "Can we make people?"

"What?"

"Artificial people."

"Where did you get that idea?"

"Mary Shelley wrote a horrific story called *Frankenstein.* I read it. It sounded possible."

"We're not sure it's impossible, yet," he answered. "There are simple robots—machines designed and programmed to duplicate the activities of humans." He thought of the vast area of biotechnology, of cloning, of artificial lungs, hearts, kidneys, prostheses—of the sea of information that had been unearthed in the years between them, wondering what he should add that might convince. He was beginning to see that this area of future wish-fulfillment could be seen as easily shammed. He needed something else, but wasn't certain what it was. It had to be something that could get to her. And in turn get him to her father.

Something occurred to him. Something mundane. "Does your father smoke?" he asked.

"A pipe. The occasional cigar. Yes."

"Tell him that tobacco crops have been replaced in the future. Tell him that there will be overwhelming evidence in the years to come that smoking is ruinous to one's health. Tell him that it is indisputably linked to numerous health disorders, including lung cancer, heart disease, emphysema."

Even in the wan light, he could see that she was alarmed. He had given her a picture close to home of her father's suffering and demise. "But," she said, "Britain has contracts with the Virginias, the Carolinas for tobacco. There are crops in Upper Canada too. You should know that."

"They will be replaced."

"By what?"

"The yellow primrose."

"What?"

"A flower that grows even now along roadsides in the Colonies and in Europe. It flourishes in the same sandy soil and climate. In my time, governments legislated the turnover in crops with little economic upheaval. Little specialized equipment or expense is needed to start production. It has similar monetary value per hectare."

"What is it used for? For decoration?"

He shook his head. "The oil is used by cosmetic manufacturers and marketed as a health-food capsule to treat ailments ranging from rheumatoid arthritis to pre-menstrual syndrome."

Rebecca said nothing.

"It's quite valuable."

Listening, she knew that he was no common criminal.

In the bushes, her mother knew the same thing.

Who was he?

Was it possible?

Harriet Anderson stepped forth into the open area beside Rebecca, startling her daughter.

"Momma!"

Christian glanced at the new figure sharply, assimilating the single word that Rebecca had used to address this woman. His mouth tightened.

Harriet Anderson stood for several moments looking not at her daughter, but at Fletcher Christian IV. His heart thumped in his chest, pumping to flood the rush of anxiety and anticipation.

The silence lengthened in the still darkness, moonlight casting shadowed fingers over them.

"Momma!" Rebecca repeated.

She ignored her daughter, fastening her gaze on the man in the circle. "Who are you?" she asked.

He paused. When he spoke, his voice was calm and low. "I'm Fletcher

Christian IV, Mrs. Anderson. I'm a traveler from the future. I'm a scientist. I've committed no crime."

"I heard you speaking with Rebecca. It's preposterous."

"But it's true." Another pause fell between them. "I need to talk with your husband further on this matter. You could be very helpful."

"You stay away from my daughter." Her voice had turned sinister.

Christian noted the shift in tone and became wary. As much as he wanted to encourage this woman to help him, he knew the fear and distrust his claim engendered in these people. The welts on his back would never let him forget.

"It was I who came to him, Momma. You know that."

Harriet Anderson finally acknowledged her daughter with a stare.

"You were listening, Momma. You know he's an educated man. I don't know what's going on any more than you do, but I know there's more to him than meets the eye!"

"What am I going to do with you? Lock you up?"

Rebecca lowered her voice. "No, Momma. But you can't lock up the truth either. The fact is that this man may not be who we think he is. It merits an investigation of some kind, don't you think? Wouldn't Father want that?"

"And what are we to tell your father? That you've been sneaking off in the night to see this man! That he told you that he's a man from the future and you want your father to look into it? Be sensible, Rebecca!"

"But you know it's not like that. You were here!"

"And you want me to stand beside you on this?"

"Tell him," said Christian, daring to interrupt, "that I would enjoy the chance to engage him in dialogue on matters of literature, history, or science. Tell him I will demonstrate to his complete satisfaction that I am not Dalton. That much I can do, at any rate. The rest of his conclusions will be his own to draw."

Harriet Anderson stared back at him.

"I have seen the future," he said.

A chill swept over Harriet Anderson. She turned, clutched her daughter by the elbow, and led her away.

When she glanced back over her shoulder, she saw that the man in the circle was lying on his back, staring up at the night sky.

34

NORFOLK ISLAND
8 July, 1835

Harriet Anderson waited until Anne had left the kitchen before going in. Drying the dishes, Rebecca turned her head when her mother entered. They were alone together.

"Your father is having a cup of tea and reading before he retires to bed."

Rebecca said nothing.

"I'm going to speak to him."

Her daughter met her eyes.

"Let me do this my way. I've given it a lot of thought. You won't be mentioned."

"Momma—"

She turned and left, leaving Rebecca standing there.

The air was heavy with the smell of pipe tobacco when Harriet entered her husband's study. Its aroma triggered the memory of the man's claim. The yellow primrose...

Her husband lifted his head from his book and smiled.

"I need to speak with you, Joseph."

"By all means, dear. Sit down." He placed his pipe in an ashtray and closed the book in his lap. It was unusual for Harriet to approach him so formally and his curiosity stirred to life, sensing his wife's anxiety the way his arthritic knee sensed a storm.

She sat on the sofa opposite his large, easy chair.

He waited. The pipe smoke curled in lazy spirals from the bowl at his right elbow.

She cleared her throat. "What are you reading? More about that ship—what was it…?"

"The *Bounty?*"

"Yes. That was it."

"No. Not right now at any rate. I'm afraid I haven't been able to get my hands on any more information regarding either Mr. Bligh or Mr. Christian."

Something twigged in Harriet Anderson's memory.

"I've finally gotten around to reading *Robinson Crusoe* by that Defoe fellow. Interesting. Bit preachy, though. He always wants to moralize about God's grand design. Ah, but it's the adventure that fixes you. Marooned, twenty-five years before seeing another man. What a tale." He shook his head with admiration. His chatter had been as much to put his wife at ease as it had been to talk about his reading matter, and they both sensed it.

Harriet, however, had heard little of what he had imparted. Her mind was clouded with what she had come to say and had then derailed onto another track with something her husband had said. She ran it through again: *Mr. Bligh or Mr. Christian…*

"What," she managed to ask, "were the names of the men on the *Bounty* that you mentioned?"

Joseph Anderson looked curiously at his wife. Such interest was unlike her. "You mean Bligh and Christian?"

"Yes. That's them. I mean," she continued, agitated, "their full names. What were they?"

"A sudden interest in British naval history, Harriet?" he asked, a tiny bit of teasing in his voice.

Her smile was nervous as her mind struggled to fit pieces together.

"William Bligh and Fletcher Christian," he said.

Harriet Anderson went cold inside.

"Dear?"

Her eyes riveted on a blank space on the wall behind him.

"What is it, Harriet?"

The memory of his words unlocked in her head. *"I'm Fletcher Christian IV, Mrs. Anderson. I'm a traveler from the future. I'm a scientist. I've committed no crime."*

"Are you all right?" He leaned toward her now.

She pulled herself from her thoughts and met his gaze.

"Harriet?"

"Yes. I'm fine."

"Are you sure?"

"Yes." She touched her forehead.

"What's this about? Is something bothering you?"

She paused. *Fletcher Christian IV.* What was happening? Her resolve hardened. "You have to do something for me, Joseph."

"What is it? What can I do?" He watched the face he had come to take for granted fill with the weight of some hidden burden.

"And I'm asking you to ask me no more than what I tell you."

He remained silent.

"No questions. Just a favor. Until this is resolved."

"Until what is resolved?"

"I need your promise."

"I don't understand."

"Your word that you will do what I request, just this once, with no questions." Her eyes were frightened.

He watched her, afraid to probe too deeply given her stance. It was completely unlike her, he knew. Something devastating was circling about in her brain, a mirror of something in her life. He thought of Rebecca and Anne. He couldn't imagine what else it could be.

"Of course," he said. "Tell me what you came to tell me. Ask what you wish."

She licked her lips. Her eyes darted about a bit before settling.

He waited.

"I want you to grant an audience to a certain prisoner. I want you to talk with him, listen to him, hear what he has to say."

He was taken aback. This was a bolt from the blue. "I don't understand."

"I can't tell you any more right now. I just need you to do this for me."

He sat stunned. "Can I ask who?"

She looked at him. "The man in the circle. The one you know as Dalton."

"Dalton!"

"Yes."

"Harriet—"

"No questions. Please."

"But how in God's name are you involved—"

"I'll tell you one thing."

He said nothing.

"I don't think he is Dalton."

One of Anderson's eyebrows rose.

"He's someone else." The fly buzzed in her brain.

"Who?"

"You ask him."

His mouth tightened.

"You'll be fascinated. I know you will."

* * **35** * *

NORFOLK ISLAND
9 July, 1835

From the position of the sun, Christian gauged it to be about nine a.m. when the two guards came for him.

"Yer lucky day, mate." The one who spoke entered the circle with a key prominent in his hand. The other man remained at its perimeter with his rifle at the ready, feet planted firmly.

"Anderson himself wants to see you. And I don't think it's to flog yer ugly hide, judging from his orders." He bent to the lock that held the chain around Christian's middle. When it turned and opened, Christian felt something akin to vertigo swim upwards from his waist to his head, and he felt literally dizzy.

"Stand up."

The chain dropped from his waist. He pushed himself first onto all fours, then up onto one knee. When he finally stood erect, he swayed momentarily, like the tall pines around him in the afternoon winds.

Free. The word rang in his brain like a clarion, drugging him with the beginnings of euphoria. *His chance. Finally.*

"Let's go." He felt the prod of the man's hand between his shoulder blades.

With unsteady steps, he crossed the rim of his own personal hell, stepping forth to the next stage of his encounter with this unpremeditated past into which he had so unceremoniously tumbled. He shuffled between his two gaolers, heading for the commandant's residence on the hill, his eyes fixed on the cannon poised so regally on the swell of lawn affronting it.

Christian was led into the room where Harriet Anderson had confronted her husband the previous evening—the room where Bran Michael Dalton had confronted the same man some months before. The room on which Rebecca Anderson had eavesdropped and where her initial curiosity about this particular prisoner had been piqued.

To Fletcher Christian IV, though, it was a brand-new setting, and one he welcomed. He glanced around, taking in the first sight of the civilized side of Empire that he had come upon since his arrival: burnished oak, a thick Indian carpet, leather upholstery, brass appointments.

And the distinctive aroma of pipe tobacco.

The man whom he assumed was Major Joseph Anderson sat behind the formidable desk, unsmiling. Christian took him to be about his own age. His face was hard, lined with experience and conviction, his graying hairline receding. Christian thought he could see the man's teeth clench and unclench as they stared at one another.

To his surprise, both Rebecca Anderson and her mother were present too, primly nervous on the settee under the window's edge. Rebecca met his eyes, briefly, penetratingly. Her mother would not.

Standing between the guards, naked to the waist, filthy and unshaven, he understood how out of place he was to the others. For the first time, too, he became conscious of his image; it had taken the change of setting to impress it upon him.

It would be an uphill battle.

Anderson took a pistol out of the bottom right-hand drawer of his desk and laid it on the top where it could be seen by all. "Leave us," said Anderson to the guards.

They nodded and backed from the room, closing the door. Anderson stared at the man. Something... Something he couldn't put his finger on... *Different...*

He cleared it from his head. "Sit down." He indicated the plain pine chair that had been placed strategically in the room's center.

Christian sat.

"I do not pretend to understand all that has transpired, Mr. Dalton, but you are here at the behest of my wife. That is the sole reason for your presence, and about the only one that I can conceive of that carried enough weight to grant you such an audience, however brief it may turn out to be. It is a tribute to my wife's common sense that I respect her sufficiently to grant a man like you any time at all. I ask that you not tax me with any form of nonsense, as I am uncertain of my patience this morning. Nor will you make any gesture or movement with any suggestion of threat or flight. If you do, I will kill you without hesitation. Is this understood?"

"Yes sir."

Anderson studied the man. "My wife and daughter are present at the request of my wife. This, too, I do not pretend to understand. But I will tell you this: I am outraged that you are somehow involved in something that has to do with my family. May God help you if you step in where you have absolutely no business. I will forget that I am a soldier, an officer, and will let you know the full measure of my wrath as a husband and father." His voice tightened with controlled anger. "Is that, too, fully understood?"

"It is."

"Good." He exhaled with pent-up exasperation. "Now what is it that you have to tell me?" The fingers of his right hand rested inches from the butt of the pistol.

For an instant the room swam with the frozen energy of the four people. Christian felt the steel of the chain that held him in the past in the eyes of the man across from him.

"I am not the man you call Dalton."

"Ridiculous." Anderson dismissed the claim with nothing more than a word and a facial expression.

"I am Fletcher Christian IV. I am from the future—the year 2072, to be exact. I am imprisoned here by accident."

Anderson's mouth turned abruptly sinister, the corners turning down. Turning to the women, he asked, "Is this your idea of a joke?"

"No!" It was Harriet who spoke for both of them. The meeting, she knew, was at its critical point already. Her husband's resentment and outrage at allowing the man to enter his quarters like this, at the inexplicable urgency of his wife, were quickly aboil. He had demonstrated, given how well she knew him, remarkable restraint in the whole matter. Now, she sensed its end. It would close like this, like a sudden roll of thunder. It was what she had feared.

Anderson turned to the prisoner, seething. "How did you get the name of Fletcher Christian?"

"Sir?"

"His name! Who told you to use it?"

"It is my name."

"Are you telling me that you are Fletcher Christian? Is that what you are actually telling me? The man is dead! If alive, he would be twice your age!"

"I am the fourth in his line to bear his name. I am his direct descendant. He is my forebear."

"Why am I sitting here listening to this?" He shook his head and looked at his wife and daughter with questioning eyes, his voice modifying.

There was silence. Both women experienced a moment of fear. How could they have been so foolish?

"The man is a charlatan or he is insane."

"I am a scientist, a man of books. Please. Ask me what you wish."

"You are claiming that you can read?"

"I can read. I welcome the opportunity to demonstrate."

"You do." Anderson's eyes narrowed. He glanced at the book on the corner of his desk. Picking it up, he weighed it thoughtfully, then leaned across the desk and tossed it toward the prisoner.

Christian caught it in both hands. Settling it on his lap, he read the spine, then opened to the title page. "How appropriate." A weak smile forced its way to his face. He looked back up at the commandant. *"Robinson Crusoe."*

Anderson muted his surprise. "I'd like to hear you read." His wariness was puzzled now.

Christian turned to the book's beginning. "'I was born in the year 1632, in the city of York, of a good family, though not of that country, my father being a foreigner, of Bremen, who settled first at Hull; he got a good estate by merchandise, and leaving off his trade, lived afterward at York; from whence he had married my mother, whose relations were named Robinson, a very good family in that country, and from whom I was called Robinson Kreutznaer; but, by the usual corruption of words in England, we are now called, nay, we call ourselves, and write our name, Crusoe; and so my companions always called me.'"

Christian lifted his head from the book to confront Anderson. The face of the commandant was filled with an expression of disbelief.

"Defoe's prose is, to my tastes, quite unsophisticated. It is a classic story, though, isn't it?" He held the book firmly in both hands. "It wasn't on any of my university courses. I read it myself, many years ago. Have you read *Moll Flanders?* Or *The Journal of the Plague Year?* Defoe excelled at the fake memoir, and helped give shape to the modern novel. It's clearly in the tradition of Bunyan's *Pilgrim's Progress* as a Puritanical allegory."

Joseph Anderson shot a glance at his wife and daughter, searching their faces for any hint as to what was happening. But they were openly rapt at the comments and mien emanating from this man. He saw no sign of any collusion.

All of which left him even further in the dark.

But the man's demonstration had altered everything. And his curious, yet astute, literary observations… *What the devil was happening?*

This man did not learn this in the slums of Dublin. No hedge school under the auspices of some drunken Papist was responsible for the quality of what he had heard here. And no Irishman was permitted by law to attend Trinity!

"What else have you read?" he asked.

"Some with which you may be familiar; much that you will not, or cannot, know."

"Tell me more."

Christian had given it much thought, and was not totally unprepared for this line of questioning. "In the field of literature, I feel reasonably conversant with the plays of Shakespeare, the works of Milton, the poetry of Donne; I am an admirer of Jonathan Swift. *Gulliver's Travels* is another that every thinking person should read. There are many similarities between it and this book here," he indicated the novel in his lap, "except that Swift was so clearly superior a mind." He paused. "Voltaire is important, too. *Candide* is a seminal work. Written, I believe, shortly after the Lisbon earthquake."

His audience remained silent.

"Even as we sit here, there is a man named Charles Darwin who will shake the roots of the scientific and philosophical world. In 1859, he will publish his *Origin of Species,* and confirm what many thinking people are already suspecting to be true—namely, that we have evolved over several millions of years to become the form of *homo sapiens* in this room. Perhaps you are familiar with one of Darwin's precursors? The French naturalist, Buffon?"

This time Anderson answered him, without realizing it. "Buffon is an interesting theorist."

"A man ahead of his time, thus generally ignored. He was the first to reconstruct geological history in a series of stages, in *Époques de la nature,* 1778; he paved the way to paleontology; he was the first to propose the theory that the planets had been created in a collision between the sun and a comet."

Anderson licked his lips. "How do you know this?"

"It is a vital part of the history of my scientific discipline. I am a professor of Life Sciences at the University of Toronto. I am president of the International Society for the Study of the Origin of Life. Buffon is a part of that tradition."

"Clearly," said Anderson, slowly, thoughtfully, "you are not who we thought you to be. You have managed to hide this erudition during your time here. Not only do I not know how this was done, even more to the point, I fail to see why it was done. Of what benefit could such deception be to you? I am clearly puzzled."

"Many things puzzle me, too. One of them is why no one can detect that I am not this Dalton. Surely, the physical resemblance cannot be that close. Although," he added, "I am developing a theory, which I would like to share with you, in good time."

"How do my wife and daughter fit into this?"

"Tell him," said Rebecca.

The two men turned to look at her.

"About the yellow primrose. How it will replace tobacco," she said.

"Perhaps at another time," said Christian.

"No," countered Anderson. "On the contrary. Tell me now. I'd like to hear what my daughter wants me to hear and what you wish to postpone telling me."

"It's just that now doesn't seem—"

"Now," said Joseph Anderson. There was still a vast area of undefined tension in the room. Christian did not wish to meddle with it unduly.

"Very well," he said. "In brief, I explained to your daughter that in my time—the future—tobacco crops have been legislated off the world market, due to the undeniable medical evidence concerning their negative health effects. They have been replaced by crops of the yellow primrose. The yield is the Vitamin E-rich primrose oil used by cosmetic manufacturers in the treatment of various and sundry health disorders, ranging from treatment of arthritis to stomach cramps to tension."

He stopped momentarily, noting their silent stares. Then he plunged on. "The turnover was complete by the middle of the twenty-first century. Using chemicals, scientists managed to convert the primrose into a plant that blooms every year; they also succeeded in developing a shatter-proof pod which prevents seed loss while harvesting. The primrose plants are grown in a ratio of 5 to 1 per acre, relative to tobacco plants. They are often grown alongside dill, coriander, and mint." He paused again. "More?"

Instead of answering, Joseph Anderson's brow knitted deeply; his eyes widened and he began to chew on the corner of his lower lip.

The women were frozen, virtually spellbound.

Christian continued. "Primrose oil is a prime source of gammalinolenic acid, which helps body tissue and cells to function. Being heat-sensitive, the methods used to extract oil from soyabean, mustard, and canola do not work for the primrose." He stopped. "You still wish to hear more? The specific dangers of tobacco? The legal and political manipulations that ensued from the death of such a major industry? The social ramifications?"

"I wish," said Anderson, "to know who you are."

Fletcher frowned. The maddening truth was that he understood the reservations that these people felt about his claims. It *was* unbelievable.

Ironically, Voltaire's words filtered into his head—that if this is the best of all possible worlds, what can the rest be like? Christian sat, genuinely befuddled at his next course of action. His audience seemed to be awaiting his next performance.

"What do you know of Fletcher Christian?" asked Anderson.

"Just about everything."

"The names of Bligh and Christian and the epic of the *Bounty* are part of the naval lore of Her Majesty's Service. What can you add?"

"If this is 1835, then you undoubtedly know of Pitcairn Island and the fate of the mutineers."

"I have made educated inquiry. I know that Pitcairn shall be their legacy and that their legacy is shame and isolation. They were madmen to do what they did. There is no escape from British justice."

"Are not their descendants innocent?"

"Do we not bear the curse of our original parents' defiance? Are we innocent of the sins of our fathers? Of the original challenge to God's authority?"

"Children of Adam," said Christian.

"Exactly."

Christian nodded, seeing that it was an area of discourse that he should not enter, an area that he could not hope to conjoin in with this man successfully. Perhaps at another time, and with great care, he thought.

"I can tell you that the population of Pitcairn over the next two hundred or so years will rise as high as 126, and as low as the present number in my own time, 21. There will be occasional emigration from Pitcairn to New Zealand, Australia, and even to Norfolk Island. I can tell you that this particular prison settlement will be gone by the latter half of this century, as will the entire practice of transportation of criminals. And I can tell you that this period and slice of British history will not make it proud in the years to come. That will be its legacy: to bear the onus and shame of colonialism to its ultimate conclusion—namely, the inevitable uprising of the ward against the parent. What happened in America was just the beginning."

"I think that is quite enough." Anderson's tone had chilled. "I wish to talk with my wife and daughter in private. But I'm sure that we will talk again." He leaned to his right and pulled a cord that hung down from the top of the wall. Behind Christian, the door opened and the two guards entered. "Escort the prisoner back to his isolation."

Christian stood up slowly from the chair, flanked by the two guards. He glanced at Mrs. Anderson and Rebecca. The look in their eyes was of a kind: confusion.

"Thank you," said Christian, "for listening. I would like to talk with you further."

Anderson worked his jaw silently. "This is not over." The words squeezed out raspingly between thin lips.

"For that," Christian said, "I am grateful."

"We shall see," said Joseph Anderson. "We shall see."

36

PITCAIRN ISLAND

7 July, 1972

"They know you're here," said Lisa.

Bran Michael Dalton looked at her warily. "Who?"

"The people in Adamstown. My parents."

He mulled this over. His home in the cave on this island called Pitcairn had been too good to be true. It had been only a matter of time.

"They know I'm meeting somebody up here. They just haven't figured out who it is yet."

"What are you going to tell them?"

"I don't know. I've been thinking about it."

"You could tell them I've been shipwrecked."

"That makes as much sense as anything else."

"Has no one ever been castaway here before?"

"I don't know I don't think so. We've had some deserters from supply ships who've hidden out until their ship leaves. But they always want to get away back to something more civilized after a while. The excitement doesn't last. Not when you're used to the things that any big city can provide."

"Maybe I could pass myself off as one of these deserters."

"The only outsiders are the RAF folks who get stationed here occasionally. They monitor the French blasts at Mururoa." Lisa became silent, thinking of John Powell, thinking of what a fool she had been. She had believed him. "They only stay a short while though. A few months at most. Then they go back to England. Or wherever."

"Could I pass as one of them?"

"Possibly. I could show you how to operate the equipment in the schoolhouse. There's been no one here since the new year." Her eyes were wistful. "John Powell wasn't replaced for four months. Another fellow was stationed here in September 1971. And he went home for Christmas. So the chances—"

Dalton stared at her as the words registered.

"What did you say?"

"Pardon?"

"Just now. When did you say the fellow was stationed here?"

"Which one?"

"The last one. Either one. I don't know."

"John Powell came in April last year. The other fellow arrived in September. His name was Edward Chapman—"

"What year did you say?"

"What do you mean what year?"

His heart was beating rapidly as the possibilities of what he thought he had heard began to register. In sympathy, his voice signaled the tension by becoming quieter. It took a moment for him to ask the question as clearly as he knew he should. He licked his lips and his eyes darted as he phrased it. "What year is this? Right now."

Lisa stared at him. "You're serious?"

He only nodded.

"You don't know?"

He said nothing.

She shook her own head. "Wow," she said. Then she gave him another long look. "It's 1972."

When he didn't respond, she asked, "You knew that, didn't you?"

"No," he said quietly. "I didn't."

"Wow," said Lisa. "Far out."

She took his hand. Dalton glanced at it, then at her, with new eyes.

1972, he thought. That was it. It explained everything. The tins of food, the soap, the sleeping bag, the radio… Good Christ!

The future…

Everything he had known—gone.

Forever.

But how did I get here?

He put his hands on Lisa's shoulders. She felt the tremor that shook him as his memories collided with the new realities of his senses. Instead of Norfolk and shackles, he felt the harshness of a Dublin winter, smelled the turf fire in the kitchen, saw his Da's weathered smile.

Gone. All of it. Irretrievably.

He had held fast to the notion that he would get back home someday, make things right. Somehow.

It was not going to happen. He knew that now.

37

NORFOLK ISLAND
10 July, 1835

"Anderson wants to see you."

Fletcher Christian IV looked up at the source of the words. At the circle's edge stood the two guards who had served as his escort yesterday.

Good, he thought. The sooner the better.

He stood and waited as the guard entered his domain to open the lock. Squinting, he fixed the cannon in his sight, admiring its endurance and strength.

Christian was standing in the hall, awaiting his audience with Joseph Anderson when Harriet Anderson came down the wide stairs. She stopped and met his eyes.

"Thank you," he said.

She did not reply. The pause was only momentary, then she continued on her way, a door closing behind her.

Christian stood between his two escorts. He waited.

"Sit down."

Christian sat in the same pine chair, in the same place, in the center of the room.

"Leave us." Anderson dismissed the guards.

When they were alone, Christian noted that the gun was also in the same place on the top of the desk, near the commandant's right hand.

Anderson studied him in silence for some seconds before speaking. "Mr. Dalton—or whoever you are—you have most assuredly given me much to think about since you sat here yesterday. And although I cannot pretend to take your claims seriously, they are not without a high degree of fascination. Among the most fascinating areas of conjecture is the simple riddle of exactly who you are, and how you ended up here. Do you wish to tell me the truth?"

"With all due respect, sir, I have told you the truth. It does sound like rather a tall tale, I must admit. And with all due respect again, sir, I understand the difficulty that you must be having in accepting it. I know that in your place, I would most likely react the same way. But it is the truth, I must stress that. No matter how unlikely, it is the truth."

"You can't expect me to accept your story."

"You must accept it. Somehow. Eventually. We cannot hide from the truth, no matter how comforting it may be to do so."

"You are suggesting that I am turning a blind eye to your 'truth'? Really… There isn't a speck of logic in anything I heard in here yesterday."

"There was a famous artist in the twentieth century, a surrealist named Dali… Did I say 'was'? My past, your future? Excuse my confusion of tenses—"

"The twentieth century is everyone's future. Even yours. Are you not here, with me?"

"Yes. You are right. But it is also my past… This does not get simpler…"

"This artist—this 'surrealist'—you were alluding to… Continue."

"A quote attributed to him that would suffice for this most 'surreal' of scenes sprang to mind. He said that to be logical is to be cuckolded every day by truth and ugliness. Your contention that my assertions yesterday were illogical does not rule out the fact that they are nevertheless true, given the nature of what has transpired."

"Of what you *say* has transpired."

Christian shrugged. "I hope to convince you. Indeed, I need to convince you. I believe my only hope of survival depends on enlisting your belief."

"One does not 'enlist' my belief, Mr. Dalton, or Mr. Christian, or whoever you are. One *shows* me, with some tangible evidence, the proof of a claim as outlandish as yours."

"I am the proof."

Anderson said nothing.

"Examine me all you will. I will hide nothing. In fact, I will disclose all, as I have willingly begun to do."

"You have engaged me in fancies. Clever ones, I admit. But fancies most assuredly."

"You flatter me. I could not dupe you, Major. What purpose could such 'fancies,' as you call them, serve? Why would I concoct such an extravagant tale?"

Anderson drummed his fingers a moment on the oak desk. "If I allow you to continue to develop this particular fancy of Man From The Future, I would be interested in hearing more about how such wise men could have bungled the exercise so cataclysmically as to have you end up here, in irons. Does not the end of the story make the story itself ludicrous?"

Christian smiled wryly. "You forget the quote from the man named Dali. Truth and ugliness assault us on a daily basis." He paused, in thought. Then, meeting the commandant's gaze once more: "You are a well-read, well-traveled man, I trust."

Anderson's expression revealed nothing.

"Yesterday, when I mentioned Buffon, you stated, if I remember correctly, that you felt him to be an interesting theorist. Does my memory serve me right?"

"It does." Anderson was intrigued.

"Buffon has been on my mind a great deal of late, as I try to sort out for myself what has happened to place me here. I think he can offer some clues for conjecture, in a mathematical framework. May I continue?"

"Please do."

"You have read Buffon?"

"Yes. At length."

"The writings as naturalist or those he penned as mathematician?"

"I have read some of the volumes from his great work, *Histoire Naturelle*. Being no mathematician myself, that area of endeavor interested me less."

"I can understand that." Christian lost himself for several seconds in reflection before continuing. "In some areas of natural science, he had a lasting influence. He was the first to present previously isolated and disconnected facts in a generally intelligible form." He smiled. "A true Renaissance man. But," he continued, "he assured himself of immortality by his discovery of a beautiful theorem in what is called Geometrical Probability."

Anderson sat, listening. He felt as if he was in the presence of a master illusionist, one whose movements were so deft and subtle as to be hypnotic.

"It is usually referred to as Buffon's Needle Theorem."

Another pause. Anderson continued to stare at him like a bird in the presence of a snake. But he was a bird with a weapon. His hand never strayed from its place beside the gun.

"We enter the area of Chance and Choice; the area of Probability. What happened to catapult me here is most certainly within this realm: a roll of the dice, the spinning of the wheel. The methods of temporal projection that we were dealing with in my century were far from tried and true. In fact, they were far from relying on known scientific knowledge." He thought of Huascar, the mystical chant, the powers of the mind. "A new area of study entirely. It is not strange that an error should occur. Trial and error are in fact part of the scientific method. And in this case, there was, I believe, a massive modifying stimulus in the form of what we call a nuclear explosion."

Christian stopped, awaiting some response.

"Go on," said Anderson.

"Do you have an atlas? Maps of the world? The South Pacific at least?"

Anderson studied him closely. Then, taking the gun in his right hand, he stood and went to the bookshelves behind his desk and extracted a large, leather-bound volume. He sat again at his desk, the volume in front of him on its large surface.

"Open it to the area of the South Pacific. Please."

As Christian watched, the pages fluttered open on the smoothed oak plane between the two men: the soft greens, muted yellows, vivid blues of cartography—the world miniaturized and sliced into graphical co-ordinates. Finally, it rested, parted on two adjoining pages with a vast expanse of vivid blue as its core.

Anderson looked up at him, waiting for this man's next bit of *legerdemain*.

"Is the west coast of South America visible on your map?"

"It is."

"Peru? Its capital, Lima?"

"Yes."

"That is where it starts. From Cuzco, actually. A bit to the south."

Anderson said nothing, listening.

"I was to be spatially, as well as temporally projected, along the latitudinal parameters within a few degrees north and south of the Tropic of Capricorn. You can see that both Pitcairn and Norfolk lie within—I would guess—five or ten degrees from the Tropic latitude. This is apparently close enough for a margin of error to be at least possible."

"Are you telling me that Pitcairn was to be your destination?"

"Yes."

"But that instead, you have arrived on Norfolk."

"Yes."

"And what year did you intend to arrive in, Mr., uh, Christian?"

The note of sarcasm did not go unnoticed. "It was expected and anticipated that I would arrive in the year 1972; since this is, in fact, 1835, as I understand it, then this constitutes the temporal error—much wider in some ways than the spatial one. I cannot account for it, as I have said. I can only assume that the synchronous explosion on July 1, 1972, in the vicinity of Pitcairn, acted as what I have termed the modifying stimulus, and deflected my path through both time and space. I am as much surprised and certainly much more chagrined than you can be."

"I'm not sure this is leading us anywhere," sighed Anderson.

"Then perhaps I should return us to Georges-Louis Leclerc, Comte de Buffon," said Christian. "His Needle Theorem."

Anderson toyed with a corner of the atlas's leather cover.

"Buffon discovered that a plane ruled with equidistant parallel lines and a needle dropped onto that plane of parallel lines would yield some fascinating mathematical results." He glanced down. "The seams on your pine floor here would suffice. Do you have a needle?"

"No."

"A matchstick would do."

Anderson hesitated before taking one from the wooden box beside his pipe and tossing it toward the prisoner. It landed on the floor between them.

"May I?" asked Christian, leaning toward the matchstick.

"You may."

"Thank you." He stepped forth from the chair, retrieved the tiny wooden segment, and returned to his seat. "If I drop this matchstick several times at random onto the pine planks of this floor, the probability that it will hit one of the lines that marks the separation seams of the boards is two times the length of this matchstick, divided by the product of the distance and *pi*, where *pi* is, of course, the ratio of the circumference of a circle to its diameter. If, in other words, we let the length of the matchstick equal *m*, and the distance between the parallel lines equal *d*, then the formula $2m/\pi d$ = Probability would illustrate the number of times that the matchstick would in actuality touch or lie across the line. Do you follow?"

Anderson frowned. "I'm not sure that it matters if I follow or not. What is this all about?"

"Just bear with me a minute more, sir. To simplify the experiment, if the length of the matchstick were equal to the distance between the lines, then the Probability of it touching the lines becomes $2/\pi$. Hence, a practical experiment involving the simplest operations, will produce the value π, which is one of the fundamental mathematical constants."

"And—?"

"And much that appears to be random to the untrained eye is, in fact, a mathematical function, governed by the immutable laws of mathematics. In 1901, the Italian mathematician Lazzerini dropped a needle 3,407 times, and obtained a value of π equal to 3.1415929, which is an error of less than 0.0000003. Even if one does not fully comprehend the full reasons for something, one may still predict with great accuracy the results — even if it *appears* to be random. Think of me as the needle, the matchstick, and the latitudinal parameters surrounding the Tropic of Capricorn as the parallel lines on this floor." Christian dropped the matchstick. "I am dropped between them; the probability that I will arrive on Pitcairn has already been determined by some law of mathematics that we have yet to discover." He bent and picked up the matchstick. "I am uncertain of the probability. Until I had tried it, it had been a 100 per cent probability. But now—" he dropped the matchstick once more. The tiny sound echoed in the still room.

"There are other factors at work here too," continued Christian. "Are you familiar with the notion of psychokinetics?"

"No," said Anderson. "I am not."

"Psychokinetics involves the power of the mind to influence an object to actually, physically, move. For instance, if I had a highly developed sense of psychokinetic power, in theory, I could influence that matchstick on the floor to move, simply by concentrating on it, by thinking it should move, by *willing* it to do so."

"Preposterous."

"Experiments were conducted at Duke University in the twentieth century, and again at Stanford in the early twenty-first. The Stanford tests gave clear evidence of some form of *pk* ability in some people—enough in many cases to significantly enhance the probability of controlling seemingly random movements—such as coin-tosses, dice rolling. Psychokinesis was also a factor in my temporal transportation here. It, too, is a science in its infancy. At any rate," he paused, knowing that only limited amounts of what he was saying could be digested by the man opposite him, "the explosion wreaked havoc on the transmission that I was involved in. The splitting of the atom is the ultimate tampering with the basic stuff of the universe. Is it any wonder that it should set me down here, in this most unlikely of places?" His voice drifted to a temporary stop, his thoughts tumbling one on another as he digested his own discourse.

"Theory. Conjecture. Mathematical pronouncement. I still have no *proof!*" Joseph Anderson's voice rose gradually. What had begun to gnaw at him was the fact that he could not *disprove* what he was hearing. If it was all sham, it was a magnificent job of forgery. This man was able to litter his account with names of places that he had never heard of, references to concepts and people that only the most learned of scholars would be familiar with, and to invest it all with an air of outrageous credibility. It was beginning to be easier to believe him than to disbelieve him, and this rankled sorely.

The commmandant glowered at his prisoner.

Fletcher Christian IV remained motionless.

"Why," asked Anderson finally, "do we not clearly recognize you as someone other than Bran Michael Dalton?" But even as he asked it, he felt a sensation like a fly buzzing in his brain, something that told him that the man here was substantially different from what he should be. It was as though some vital memory was missing, but he could not pin it down.

"That," answered Christian, "is a very good question. Perhaps it is the key question, for if I could answer it, I would understand exactly what has happened here. If you could see clearly that I was not the same man that you had locked up, then my case would be immeasurably simpler to plead. But this lack of recognition, this situation where the memory of Dalton's physical presence has been erased from everyone's mind, is the ultimate complication. Could you stand another theory or two?"

"I *need* another theory or two in order to approach even the remotest possibility of believing your fantastic tale!"

Christian nodded slowly. "We all need theories. And then we hope that we will be fortunate enough to live long enough to see one of them validated." He smiled weakly. "Occasionally, it happens. Would that it will happen in this instance."

"If you were not Dalton, I would know it. Is it not that simple?"

Christian shrugged. "But that is not the case. So, we must speculate why. Why, indeed?" He paused. "It is possible that this Dalton character has been transported to Cuzco or Pitcairn in my place. My presence here, and the fact that no one can see that I am not Dalton, indicates that it is as though Dalton's physical appearance and identity is of no particular consequence in the large scheme of things, as they exist over a span of millenia. It is an idea that holds some interesting philosophical truth— that a thing's, or a person's, appearance is of little or no consequence in the grand scheme of things. It is what a person does, what a thing's function is, that is of importance—how it interacts with the environment that will be its sole legacy—the function that we serve as minuscule links in the chain of reproduction and interaction throughout the scores of centuries—*this* is what is important. If this is so, then it is our function that is of import, not our appearance. If we were to be perceived as other persons completely, somehow the chain would have been broken too stridently. Its shattering would have ramifications in Time that we can only wonder at."

Anderson was content to listen. In fact, he was rapt.

"Another possibility is that my coming here has, literally, changed *everything*—changed it in ways so profound that we cannot guess the potential circles of consequence throughout history. This would include the altering of memories of people to coincide with the smooth chain of events that was somehow unfolding. For people to clearly recognize the fact that their world has ruptured open, that the fabric of linear Time has been rent, much like we managed to rend the atom itself, may not allow for whatever was to be the destiny of Man. It may be Time's, or God's, or the Universe's—whatever label one wishes to apply—way of proceeding to its ultimate goal, be that what it may. Perhaps there *is* a master plan. Perhaps your failure to recognize that I am not Dalton is part of it. Perhaps our dialogues, my stay here…perhaps these are necessary things on the march through Time toward a manifest destiny. I don't know."

For the first time, Joseph Anderson stood up and took his eyes off the prisoner. He stared at the shelves beside him without focusing, deep in thought.

"Or perhaps Time and Space and the nature of Reality are much more complex than we can imagine: This may not be a true past; it may be an alternate past, an alternate time-track. It is not altogether a novel idea. It has occurred to both scientists and fantasists for centuries."

Anderson looked at him sharply. "What do you mean, this may not be a *true* past! Are you suggesting that my life is any less real than yours?" Even as he asked the question, both of them realized that it indicated a willingness to discuss the matter as a legitimate possibility. No longer was

Christian's tale being dismissed outright. Joseph Anderson was finally struggling openly with the possibility that the tale he had been presented with might be true. It was a startling revelation for the commandant himself, and a welcome one for Fletcher Christian IV.

For the first time, too, Anderson paid little heed to the pistol on his desk. A gunshot would not solve this mystery. Nor did this man strike him as a killer—a breed to which his instincts had been honed sharply over the years.

"I did not express myself well," said Christian quietly. "I was merely suggesting that it was possible to speculate that this was not a true *linear* past of the world from which I came. I may have shifted into an alternate past, one with a completely different set of futures, or, indeed, with a future that no longer contains *me*. After all, how could it, if I were, against all hope, never to return to my own Time? As I said, the possibilities remain endless in the absence of solid data or firsthand experience."

"Parallel lines in Time," muttered Anderson. "Like your latitudinal parameters along the Tropic of Capricorn." He was rambling aloud now, working out ideas that were as new as seedlings sprouting from soft loam. His face was animated with the unorthodoxy of his thoughts. "Universes and timelines pressed together like sheets of paper." Then he paused, seemed to regain some of his former composure. "This is madness. You've even got me listening to this nonsense!" He leaned forward, hands on his desk, confronting Christian. But there was a trace of fear, of awe in his visage, an expression that had only been born in this room within the last few minutes. Christian noted it well.

"There is one other thing."

"And that is?"

"Either your wife or your daughter has an article of clothing that I gave them for their examination. A shirt. If you would be so kind as to ask them for it, you could make a study of it yourself. It is a fabric and design unknown to this era."

Anderson stared at him wide-eyed.

"Ask for it. Study it."

Anderson said nothing for a long time. Then: "I will do that, sir." Reaching for the cord hanging on the wall, he fixed his gaze on the disheveled man of learning, gaunt and haggard in the chair before him. Before pulling the signal cord, Anderson spoke again. "You will be sent back to the general prisoners' barracks. Your period of isolation is, for now, terminated."

Christian was certain that the gratitude was unmasked on his face. "Thank you."

"For now."

"I understand."

"And you will cause no further trouble."

"I have caused none yet. I am not Dalton."

Anderson pulled the cord. Within seconds, the two guards arrived. Christian pushed himself to his feet and stood in the middle of the room. Anderson stared back at him.

"I will summon you again, shortly."

"Yes sir."

"Return the prisoner to the barracks instead of the isolation circle."

The guards glanced at one another; then the larger of them said, "Yes sir."

Anderson watched them leave before crossing the room and closing the door. Then he stood at the window and watched them as they crossed the compound. It took until they had disappeared from view that he felt his pulse slow back to normal, and he felt his breathing resume comfortable rhythms.

Was it possible? He didn't know. But he did know where he was going now. To find his wife. To ask about the shirt.

To see for himself.

* * 38 * *

NORFOLK ISLAND
10 July, 1835

Fletcher Christian IV was left in the care of yet another guard at the prisoners' barracks—a large, unkempt, burly man with a protruding gut and
a ragged scar on his left cheek. When his two escorts had departed, the
man turned to Christian, grunted, and eyed him condescendingly before
he spoke. "You must've kissed the Major's bloody arse, my Irish friend, for
him to cut your stay in the circle short. Fuckin' black magic, it is, for him
to administer leniency of any sort—especially to an arsehole the likes of
you." He spat on the floor, oblivious to the obscenity of the action. "But
we still want to see to it that you don't miss anything exciting here at the
bottom, so it's off to the kilns with the others for you. I'm sure you've
missed the good honest labor." He smiled maliciously.

"What's at the kilns?" Christian asked.

The guard's right eyebrow rose curiously. Then he began a slow, deci-
sive stroll around the prisoner, stopping when he arrived behind him.
Then, swiftly and viciously, he kicked Christian with the full blow of his
boot in the calf. Christian's mouth opened in surprise and pain, and he
buckled to one knee, his eyes watering.

"God knows why the commandant let a smart arse like you off so easily." The man's voice dripped his contempt. "What do you fuckin' well think is at the kilns? A fuckin' tea party?" He stared down at the man.

Christian was gasping to keep the pain under control.

"Smart fucker, aren't ya?"

Christian knew better than to answer. He continued to gasp for air. His brief interval with Anderson had let him forget the reality of Norfolk.

The reality of pain.

"Get up."

Christian forced himself up, wavering. He could not place any weight on his right leg.

"Let's go," the man said.

Christian hobbled, limping, toward the door.

"To the fuckin' tea party," he said.

The walk had taken a painful ten minutes. And each time he had slowed down, the guard had prodded Christian with less and less gentle jabs with his rifle butt in the small of Christian's back. Combined with the aching throb from the bruised muscles in his right calf, Christian once again waded through a variation on the sea of physical torment that washed this island in a constant tidal flow.

They emerged into a clearing—a white-dusted quarry area, with wheelbarrows, canvas sacks, picks, shovels, and about a dozen ashen-faced men who stopped to gaze at the new arrivals. There were three guards seated on large rocks at the perimeters of the clearing, enclosing the prisoners in a triangular pattern. A few hundred meters farther, Christian could see a wooden building; its two chimneys poured forth steady streams of white smoke.

Even at this distance, Christian could see the lime in the wheelbarrows, see it puffing from the tops of the open sacks, see its ghostly pallor on the faces and arms and backs of the men.

"See," said the man behind him. "They're havin' their afternoon tea!"

The guard nearest, who had been within earshot, laughed aloud.

Squinting, Christian made out the movement of other men in and around the wooden building which housed the kilns. They had not yet noticed this small intrusion.

"This man would like a cup in her majesty's finest bone china," said the escort.

"Blimey," said the guard who had laughed. "You've brought us the fuckin' madman from the circle!"

"And a right gen'leman he is, too." He jabbed him with the rifle butt between his shoulder blades, sending him forward into the open for all to see. Then, because he was still standing, he strode up to him and struck him viciously with the rifle in the small of the back. Christian shook and dropped to his knees with a muffled cry, the pain searing him with silent shock. Gasping for breath, he fell forward onto his hands, trying to hold himself from total collapse while his body assimilated this latest assault.

"Yes," said the guard who had played the foil for the large-gutted man. "He's a real gen'leman, he is." He moved from the rock where he had been sitting and walked the dozen feet to where the prisoner had fallen, clutching handfuls of sand in shaking fingers in an effort to squeeze the pain from his body.

"A real gen'leman." The other prisoners and guards had all stopped to watch the spectacle that they sensed was about to be played out. The guards let smiles slide onto their faces; the prisoners forced their faces to remain impassive.

They all watched.

Standing over the fallen prisoner, the guard unbuttoned the front of his pants with his left hand; his right hand held the rifle, buttressed in his armpit. Taking his penis from his pants, he urinated on the man at his feet. "Welcome," he said, "to the tea party."

Laughing, the burly escort turned and left.

In silence, the prisoners watched them go.

* * **39** * *

NORFOLK ISLAND
10 July, 1835

Major Joseph Anderson stared at the magical labels inside the collar of the strange shirt in his hands. *Bahru Menswear, Singapore.*

Singapore!

Good Lord, thought Anderson. How does a common Dublin criminal end up with such a garment?

And he knew again that the man who called himself Fletcher Christian IV was not a common Dublin criminal. Everything cried out that he was not.

Everything except common sense.

And what the devil was polyester?

He looked up into the faces of his wife and daughter, who had been watching him. And when they saw his eyes, they knew that he had finally accepted what was happening. What they knew, with an intuition beyond femininity, was as true as a knife-stroke into their collective vitals.

The future in the past.

In his mind, a surreal mélange of images juxtaposed themselves. He saw the needle in Time, the *Bounty* sailing seaward, and conjured up an explosion that he did not understand. Mathematics, rebellion, and some primal force out of nightmare had conspired to force the truth front and center—to visit it at the core of his family and life, at the deepest well-springs of his own truths.

Happenstance or design?

He did not know.

Nor did he know how to find out.

40

PITCAIRN ISLAND
8 July, 1972

"Who's the king of England?" asked Bran Michael Dalton.

"It's a queen. There's no king." Lisa bored her bright eyes into his.

"Victoria?"

"No. Elizabeth. Elizabeth II. It's on all the stamps and coins."

He mulled this over.

She giggled.

"What's so funny?"

"You are. The questions you ask. I can't believe it."

"Do you have a stamp or a coin? Something I could see?"

"I think so." She pulled her bag to her and rummaged about, finally extracting a brown leather wallet. She undid a small snap and took out a silver coin, handing it to him.

He took it in his fingers, letting his thumb read its inscription with circular caresses. Then he held it closer and stared at it as if it were a rune. And although he could not read, he was not unintelligent; he had managed to build up a formidable degree of simple word-recognition as a survival tool. Money was one of the things he could "read" with relative ease.

"It's a shilling," he said.

She nodded.

He read the date. "1949."

"It's not a new one."

He turned it over, looked at it, then at her. "You said you had a queen."

"We do."

"There's a man on the back."

She took it from him, examined it. "He must have been king before her," she said. "I don't know." She read around the edge of the coin. "It's Latin. But it says *George VI*. I can read that much." She handed it back to him. "I've got others." She jingled coins in the wallet's pouch for a moment. A larger, copper coin surfaced in her fingers. "A penny," she said.

He took it. It was indeed a penny. The date this time read 1961. He rolled it over in his fingers.

There was a woman on its obverse.

Lisa watched his eyes. "That's Queen Elizabeth." She tapped the miniature engraving with her finger. "See," she said. Her finger traced the inscription. "Elizabeth II." She sat back, satisfied.

Dalton could not read the inscription. But he knew that it said what Lisa claimed it said. He had seen the dates. *1949. 1961.*

A sudden fire lit in his eyes. He stared at her hard. "And Ireland," he said. "What about Ireland?" He seemed to be smoldering.

She saw the change. "I don't know, Bran. I mean, I don't follow that kind of stuff much—history, news. We don't get newspapers regularly. And," she apologized, "I'm not a very good reader." Then she brightened. "But I hear things on my radio. I think there's fighting there. A war or something." She frowned. "Belfast's in Ireland, isn't it?"

He nodded, soberly. "It is." In the dreaded North, he thought.

"People get killed there. I don't know what's happening."

Her words upset him. "And in Dublin?"

"I don't know."

But they're all dead and gone, he tried to remind himself. All of them. It doesn't matter what's happening there now *Mary Mullan. Jenny. Sandy-haired Maag on the quays. Da.* His eyes clouded.

Then he thought of himself, here, unchained.

Why? he thought.

If I'm free, why do I feel so empty?

Lisa's hand reached across to stroke his brow. Her fingers cooled him and he shivered.

When they made love later, neither had the presence of mind to use a condom. The idea did filter into their passion, but only as a wisp of smoke amid the blaze, quickly consumed and obliterated.

Driven, he sought a kind of extinction in the pounding of the blood, and Lisa welcomed him.

And another seed was cast onto the winds of Time.

41

NORFOLK ISLAND

12 July, 1835

Percy Teversham had watched Bran Michael Dalton in silence for the past two days, alert and curious beneath his wrinkled brow and his ever-present sty.

Something was amiss. He didn't yet know what it was. But there was something.

Bran didn't know him anymore. There was no recognition whatsoever.

They had done something to him. His mind had snapped. Percy had seen it before.

Gone too was the palpable air of rebellion that had accompanied Dalton like a cloak of many colors. He was quiet. Broken.

Percy could understand.

And yet…

And yet there was something else. The others seemed to sense it as well.

It was crazy. Percy knew that. But then, everything was crazy here on Norfolk. It was like…

He couldn't quite put a coherent thought around the notion. It flitted at the recesses of his brain, shaping itself, then was gone, a wisp, uncatchable.

It was like Dalton had been excised from existence, replaced by this other Dalton, this peaceful, accommodating man who spent most of his time observing and meditating.

But Percy knew the notion was madness. The reality was simple.

They had succeeded. They had broken him.

And Percy felt the defeat in his own soul.

Staring at Bran Michael Dalton, he felt something like a fly buzzing in his brain, and searched, without realizing it, for the missing data that would make this man intelligible to him. But there was nothing.

16 July, 1835

It had been six days since Dalton had been returned to the barracks. They slept on the floor on their backs. There was no turning over, no tossing about; this was predicated by the steel bar that was slid through their leg irons, clamping them in place for the night. Eventually, they slept from sheer exhaustion.

Percy Teversham touched the sty on his eyelid with the fingers of his left hand as he lay on his back in the darkness. Then he did the same with the fingers of his right hand.

The fear crawled freely within him.

It was getting worse.

Every night he repeated the process. And every night he was more sure.

If the guards found out, that would be it.

And they would find out. Everyone would. Eventually.

22 July, 1835

Fletcher Christian IV had been assimilated into the twenty men that formed his communal bloc. They crossed paths constantly, working, eating, sleeping, voiding their wastes… Privacy was a memory, like so many other things. He had no idea how many prisoners were on the island.

Certainly hundreds. Perhaps it ran between one and two thousand. It was possible. But there was communication only within the block in which one was situated. The others remained mere visual entities, ghost-forms with sunken chests and shuffling gaits, engaged in any variety of demeaning labor—from digging cesspools to clearing rocks from the fields. Christian had gathered that the more senior prisoners—survivors of note—were usually assigned more civilized tasks. If there was a reward for longevity and endurance, that seemed to be it.

It was in the darkness that night that Christian first heard about it. The traversing bar had been slid into place; most of the men were prone on their backs, exhausted. The mosquitoes droned their annoyance in the still, warm air. A few men sat upright, quiet, for this was a form of solitude for them, the moment when they were finally left alone for the day.

"We need witnesses," said a voice.

Christian pushed himself up onto one elbow and squinted into the gloom. The shapes of the others took form in the dimness. Everyone was propped up in some fashion, staring at the voice.

It was the man he knew as Bates.

"We've made a pact." Bates nodded to the man beside him. "Me and Fallon. Right, Fallon?"

"Aye."

Christian had not heard the man speak before. Glancing to his own left, Christian met the gaze of the elfin man with the outrageous sty over his eye, the man he knew as Percy. "What's he talking about? What's going on?" His voice remained barely audible.

The man watched him for a moment. "It's like he said," came the thick, dockside accent. "A pact."

"What's a pact?"

Percy stared at him. He doesn't know, he realized. "They draw straws," he said. "They've agreed."

"Agreed to what?"

"To a solidarity pact. The one who gets the short straw kills the other one."

Christian said nothing for a moment. Then: "I don't understand."

Percy Teversham looked at him. "What's to understand? One to die, the other to kill him. The rest of us as witnesses." He coughed violently, then had to let his lungs clear the phlegm before continuing. "It's their choice," he said.

"What kind of choice is that? Are they crazy?"

Percy listened to the wild note in the man's voice, realized how much he had forgotten. Or changed. "Neither of 'em want to go on." He shrugged. "So what? It's an act of solidarity. We support it. You could be wantin' it next. Maybe me." He shrugged again.

"It's suicide."

Percy said nothing.

"They'll hang the one who does the killing! What's the point?"

"The killer will be sent to Sydney for trial. Gives him two chances—he can try to escape in transit; lots more opportunities than here. Or else he'll be freed by hanging."

Christian had no response.

"Sometimes it's better," said Percy. "We each of us makes up our own minds about it."

"This is insane!"

Percy turned to stare at him, puzzled.

"Witnesses." The voice came out of the darkness.

Two or three of the men signaled the beginning of general assent with muttered "ayes;" in staggered succession, other ritualistic "ayes" followed. Then there was a moment of tense silence.

"I've the straws here," said Bates. He held two sticks of pine twig in his hand, one about six inches, the other short by an inch or two. "Percy," he said. "You do it."

Careful to use his right hand, Percy reached out and took the straws from the man who had crawled forward to hand them to him. At the limit of his extension, he heard Bates's chain pull taut against the traversing bar. Then Bates sat back while the others watched the twigs in Percy's hand. The pieces of twig drew their eyes like magnets.

"I'll draw," said Fallon.

Christian saw the man's eyes like moons in the fetid room.

Shielding the straws from the sight of all, Percy Teversham nestled them arbitrarily in the palm of his hand. Then he brought them forth, holding them aloft, his fist a grim chalice.

Christian watched it all in horror: another layer of nightmare peeled back.

In his mind's eye, he saw the scene superimposed on a tableau from memory. *Haucaypata Square. Huascar's hands raised aloft.*

From the scrawny hand the two sprigs jutted ominously. Life and Death.

Fallon crawled forward. He chose. It trembled in his fingers.

The long straw.

Percy opened his hand and the short straw fell out.

All eyes went to Fallon. To the one who would be killed by his mate.

"It's best," said Fallon.

No one else said anything.

Fallon leaned back and put his hands behind his head, staring into the darkness above.

"This is madness!" said Christian.

Percy looked at him dolefully. "Yes," he said. "It is. All of it."

"You can't let this happen!"

"For Christ's sake, man! Calm yourself!" Percy's words cut the silence.

Christian heard him and tried to control his ragged breathing. His mind reeled. *This is too much,* he thought. *I can't deal with it any more.*

There was a quick movement across from him, then a groan. "What's happening?" Christian peered into the gloom.

The groan continued for a few seconds, then ceased. He saw Fallon's legs spasm and twitch, then become still.

"It's done," whispered Percy.

"What's done, for God's sake?"

"Are you an idiot, man? Keep quiet!"

Christian stared across at Fallon, then back at Percy. "He killed him? Just like that?"

Percy ignored him.

"But just like that?" He didn't know exactly what it was that he wanted to ask. Did he want to know more of the rules of this bizarre pact? The murder weapon? But he also knew that his questions went far beyond the details of this scenario. They went to the core of everything.

"Why wait? You decide, you decide. Would you like to lie awake all night thinking about it? Not me." Percy paused. Then he nodded in Fallon's direction. "Not him, either."

The others had already settled back for the night. Stunned, Christian too lay back. In the darkness, his eyes darted and his face muscles jumped. Finally, in spite of himself, tears streamed down both sides of his face.

And in the darkness, a new smell intruded.

The smell of death.

Christian felt it settle into the room's putrid corners, creep into his clothes and skin like a damp mist, and embrace him with its foul breath.

Unholy lovers, they shared the night.

With the light of dawn came the flies. They buzzed and fed on the stink of the corpse.

The bile rose from Christian's innards regularly as the hours passed.

Then came the guards. There was little commotion—a few gruff shouts of disgust and accusing questions. All were silent as Bates confessed. The guards kicked him and struck him repeatedly as they led him away, more upset at the trouble he had caused than anything else. Then they fell to the grisly task of moving the body, and spat and cursed at the thing that had once been a man.

Christian saw it all.

When they returned to the remaining men and began unlocking them from their nocturnal fetters, Christian waited until the others were out of earshot before turning to the nearest guard. "I want to see Major Anderson," he said.

The man squinted at him. "And what makes you think he wants to see you?"

"Just tell him that the man called Dalton or Christian wishes an audience. He'll be interested. He'll thank you." Christian stared him down.

The guard stared back at the prisoner. There had been rumors about this one. Something had gone on up at the commandant's house, and suddenly this one had been freed from isolation. He didn't know what it was, but he did know that this may be a special case. He was not that stupid.

"I'll tell him," he said.

They left, heading for the kilns. The sun was already hot.

42

NORFOLK ISLAND
23 July, 1835

The other prisoners watched curiously when the two guards came for Christian. It was shortly after noon, shortly after the slops that passed for lunch. Percy Teversham, in particular, watched the man being escorted away. His left hand hung at his side, the fingers useless.

The fly buzzed in his brain.

In the commandant's office, in the pine chair, Christian stared at Anderson.

"I've thought about you a great deal, Mr. Dalton, or Mr. Christian, or however you choose to call yourself. What can I do for you now?"

"A man was killed where I slept last night."

"Yes. I know. We have his murderer."

"Do you know why he was killed?"

"Does it matter?"

"Don't you care?"

"Not really. Anger. Frustration. A debt. Violent men will do violent things. These things happen."

"The two men swore a suicide pact. A solidarity pact. One to kill, the other to be killed, determined by chance."

Anderson pursed his lips. "I've heard of these things. What would you have me do?"

"Does it not bother you that men would choose death over life here?"

"Not at all. Given their predicaments, I might consider the same options."

"But you are the commandant of the island. Surely, you are concerned at the way the men perceive it here!"

"Indeed, I am. And I take it well that they dislike being here so thoroughly. Word will spread to others. Transportation is to be a deterrent to the criminal, to temper his views, to make him think twice."

"But it didn't work, Major."

"What didn't work?"

"Transportation as deterrent."

"I forgot. You're from the future. You know these things." The sarcasm was evident.

"There will come a time when the term Industrial Revolution will be commonplace. It refers to the movement of a society like England's from an agrarian one to an urban one. In England now, due to the blinkered myopia of some of its leaders, population, poverty, alcoholism, and crime rates are out of control. Prison hulks are bursting with felons. Where to send them? To the human trash heap—Australia—to purge England of a whole class, the criminal class—sweep it under the rug. A whole continent, along with its islands, as a jail, with vast seas for walls. But no one faced the root causes of the geometric rise in criminality: unemployment and hunger, byproducts of the industrial age."

"And you know all this."

Christian bored his gaze into the man's eyes. "You know I do."

Anderson said nothing. I'm not sure, he thought. He might know. He just might.

"Transportation will last for about thirty more years. Aborigines will be exterminated. A legacy will be passed on."

"What legacy? Does Australia become the cesspool of the future, the genetic wasteland of the future? I cannot see how it could be otherwise, if the place were to breed the scum that fill its prisons."

"In fact, Major, one of the most intriguing developments in Australian study is how the post-colonial land failed to reflect its criminal origins. From a community of people, handpicked over decades for criminal propensities, came one of the most law-abiding societies in the world. From parents and grandparents, dark and stunted products of slums and mills, will come children well-fed, cradled in sunshine—fair-haired, blue-eyed, tall, and straight. The theory of genetic criminal inheritance will be exploded. It is a myth. There is no such thing as a criminal gene. Criminals cannot be grouped. Each one is an individual case. Some are beyond reclamation; some are not. As someone whose life has been spent, and will be spent, in this discipline, it should be of primary importance to you to distinguish between two such people, to be able to mete out justice with greater fairness and wisdom."

Anderson's temper was simmering at the man's affront. "You sit there and condemn me and my efforts."

"Not you. Not your efforts. The results of your efforts, yes. I condemn this—" he spread his hand in an expansive sweep, indicating the camp, the island, everything that surrounded them.

"You're an imposter."

"You know I am not."

The two men stared at each other.

"I am the future."

Anderson breathed heavily. He could not decide what to do with this man. He challenged everything.

"You could be a pioneer, a visionary." Christian paused. "There is no need for any of this. History will tell."

Because his curiosity was greater than his anger, Anderson probed further. "You have a vested interest in this line of thinking, is that it?"

"I don't understand."

"For the sake of argument, say you actually are Fletcher Christian IV, descendant of the mutineer. What I am hearing is merely a form of self-

assurance that you do not carry any of his dissident genes within you. You, too, are the descendant of a criminal, one lionized in the annals of naval history. Does it make sense for you to argue other than you have?"

"This is not about me."

"On the contrary, everything is about ourselves, ultimately. You claimed to be seeking your own ancestors, were you not? Trying to determine where you came from? To see first-hand what seeds spawned you? And what has become of the society that Fletcher Christian and his barrel-bottom cohorts procreated?"

Christian took a moment for reflection. He thought about the kernels of truth in the Major's observations. "Pitcairn remains a static society, inbred, God-fearing. It, too, makes the point I have been expressing. In the sense that we should feel responsible for the crimes—sins, if you will—of our forefathers, there simply is no Original Sin. Each of us is born with a clean slate. We are all responsible for ourselves. Our morality is not inherited at large. There may be recessive genes for anything down through the centuries; but they are merely part of the lottery of life. I am sure, Major, that a thorough and incursive investigation into even your own illustrious ancestry would uncover a sheep-stealer or two."

"Your boldness may be unwise."

"My desperation shows me new resolution. I can see no other way."

"There is no room for violence in your philosophy? You are unable to comprehend one man killing another?"

"On the contrary, invasion and conquest were going on long before any creature was sophisticated enough to think of violence as a tactic. The earliest living organisms fought each other. The bacteria that may give you a sore throat are like cousins a million times removed. The bacteria simply come from a line of the life chain that didn't evolve in as complex a way as we did. And when you take medicine for a cure, it might be called an obscure form of fratricide. Cells have always lived on other cells, invading them, consuming them. Blind survival and conquest. We eat other cells, plant or animal. But torture and punishment of the body and the mind—these are the machinations of Man. And they are philosophically lurid and repulsive beyond belief."

"You do not believe in execution for murderers?"

"Elimination of specific unpleasant and harmful organisms can have its place in a society. It is not done lightly."

"You are here to plead for this man, Bates? This murderer in your barracks?"

"On the contrary, he wishes to die. I am here merely to ask you to consider what it is that you do that makes him harbor such a wish, unnatural as it is, and unproductive as it will prove."

"Control is the operative word here. We must have control or anarchy will prevail, Mr... Christian."

"To control, you must break these men."

"Yes."

"It is a waste."

They eyed one another with wariness.

"A waste," he repeated.

Anderson watched the man, articulate beyond anything he as commandant or world-traveler had experienced before. "Do you not wish," he said, "that you could go back to your own time, Mr. Christian?"

Christian's eyes fogged. "Yes," he said.

"But you do not know how."

"No," he said. "I do not."

"It is too bad," said Anderson. "Because I do not know what to do with you, either." He reached for the cord to summon the guards. The audience was at an end.

"You will be back. You are the most stimulating conversationalist I know."

* * 43 * *

NORFOLK ISLAND
21 August, 1835

I'm here, thought Christian, *and it looks like I'm going to stay here.*

A month had passed since his confrontation with Joseph Anderson concerning the Bates-Fallon pact. And rumor had it that at least one other pact had been carried out in another block since then.

Intermittent blips of despair on a line graph of mindless resignation, he thought. And we go on. We go on.

We try to go on.

Inching into the future with glacial slowness, blinders on every side.

It was dark in the barracks. Christian sat forward on his haunches, inured to the stink of sweat and unwashed bodies around him. The air in the closed space was thick and stale, and mosquitoes buzzed monotonously, the only sound in the humid, still room. His scalp itched and his stomach growled with incessant hunger. Too tired to move, he could only stare at the bar that held his legs in place for the night.

Liana. Toronto. Singapore. Lima. Cuzco. Liana.

Memories.

The thick air was like water slipping through his nose and into his lungs. For a moment he thought he was drowning. Everything shimmered, then steadied.

Slowly, he turned his head and stared at Percy Teversham, whose skeletal shape lay unmoving beside him. The sty on his eye was enormous—a grotesque thing that kept his lid shut at all times now. There was no treatment. No one cared.

But there was more to Percy's illness than the sty. Christian had been watching him. The man's lips were breaking out in sores that Christian had never seen before, and Christian sensed that the sty was merely another manifestation of this undercurrent of poison that glided morosely and invisibly through the man's veins.

And Christian had seen something else. Percy could no longer use his left hand. Something was wrong with the nerves or muscles there. The hand seemed dead.

He's dying, thought Christian, bit by bit. Not all at once, like Fallon. In pieces.

The others did not speak of it, if they noticed.

It went beyond courtesy. It was based on fear.

They saw themselves in him.

19 September, 1835

"It has been a while, Mr. Christian."

Seated in his pine chair, he gazed at Joseph Anderson. "I cannot believe, Major, that you still find my story, when combined with my knowledge, demeanor, and supporting evidence, to be so unconvincing as to merit no further investigation. Frankly, I would have expected either much more dialogue between you and me to confirm what I have told you, or simply that you would release me, since at the very least it is clearly a case of mistaken identity."

"I have no idea who you are."

"I have told you."

"Or what you are."

"You seek intrigue and deception where there is none. As an English writer from the latter half of this century put it: when you have eliminated the impossible, what remains, no matter how improbable or unlikely, must be the truth."

"The impossible is that you are from the future. The more I mull it over, the more fantastic it is. I have come, though, to admire your flair. Your tale is the boldest I have ever encountered."

"The impossible is that I am Bran Michael Dalton."

Anderson took his spectacles off and placed them on the desk in front of him.

Christian's own eyes narrowed as he stared at them. "Reading," said Anderson, "ultimately inflicts its toll."

"Myopia?"

"Pardon?"

"Near-sightedness?"

"Yes. Reading combined with advancing years. And trying to see through tall tales." He smiled. "How, uh, is such a problem dealt with in the marvelous world of the future—the world free of the short-sightedness that you see everywhere about you?"

Christian hesitated. Then he bore on. "Laser light is used in most cases to reshape the cornea. It's called photorefractive keratectomy. An extremely thin layer is skimmed off the cornea, the transparent cover through which light travels. It's at the atomic level of removal— 25/1,000ths of a millimeter or so."

Anderson stared at him in silence for several seconds. "Have you had this done?"

"No. I'm comfortable with eyeglasses. In my time, I'm an anachronism."

"Ironic, wouldn't you say?"

"Yes, I would say."

"And another fascinating story."

Christian was quiet for a second. "How can I convince you?"

"I don't know."

Christian shifted in his chair. "I came to see you about a man who is sick. A man who needs help."

"We all get sick."

"This man is dying."

"Then what can I possibly do for him?"

"You could treat him humanely. You could ease his suffering."

"Where do you think you are, Mr. Christian?"

"I thought I was in the presence of an intelligent, educated man. And I assumed that these were qualities that would permit you to address something as obvious as this."

"Address it how?"

"Establish a hospital. Offer some form of medical care."

"This is a prison."

"In my time the two concepts are not exclusive."

Anderson breathed with some exasperation. "Your veiled lectures about the barbarism that you see about you are beginning to annoy me. If I am near-sighted, then so are you. This is a penal institution, Mr. Christian. A *penal* institution. Do you understand the word? Comforts and pleasures have been forfeited. They exist for those who have not broken the laws that we are all bound by."

"And basic human rights? How have they been forfeited?"

"A fine and noble phrase, that: basic human rights. Like a Daniel, you sit in judgement! And what is this you have told me about this future world that is so grand and compassionate? You arrived here, you tell me, as the result of an explosion of a magnitude that can warp time and space, if I understand you. Is this explosive device the result of advancement in the noble concept of 'basic human rights?' Or have I misunderstood some of your tale—real or imagined?"

Anderson's nostrils were flared. "Basic human rights," he muttered, putting his spectacles back on. "I'll tell you what I see, my judgmental, righteous prophet. I see a man who does not understand where he is! I see a man who is so near-sighted that he thinks a purported Man From The Future can step into a past he has not lived in and apply the latest philosophical sentiments and sit back smugly and contemplate his 'improvements'!"

"We evolve, both as a physical species, and philosophically."

"You know, Mr. Christian, I *do* listen to you. And it was you who told me that we evolved over millions of years. *Millions,* you said. And contrary to whatever conceit or vanity you may hold about yourself, I do not yet perceive you as a significant step forward in evolution. And I find your judgment of me and my lifework both presumptuous and condescending."

"The man is dying."

"We are all dying, Mr. Christian."

"He can be comforted."

"Then comfort him. Appease your conscience—that vast moral arbiter that you would share with me. *I* understand what I am doing here, even if you do not. This is my life. I am not a visitor."

Christian sat in silence, letting Anderson's words wash over him before they drained away. Then he nodded, slowly.

Maybe, he thought, it's my life too. Maybe I should stop thinking about my life as something else, and this as some rude break in its flow.

This, he thought, is it. Get on with it. Live it.

They stared at one another.

24 October, 1835

"What's the matter, Percy?" Christian asked finally.

The little man gazed out from his one good eye at the man walking beside him. They would be at the kilns in less than five minutes. The guards were out of earshot.

"What do you mean?"

"You're sick. Your left hand. Your eye. Your…face, lips…."

Percy touched his lips and chin absently as they plodded along. A minute went by before he answered. He said, "Must be the good, clean livin'." Beneath the red, raised nodules on his lips, he smiled a death-grin.

But he said no more.

18 November, 1835

In the dank, sweaty stillness of night, lying cloistered with the foul stench of the others, Fletcher Christian IV sat up slowly and noiselessly. He stared down at the sleeping form of Percy Teversham beside him.

And suddenly understood.

The man's eye was virtually gone; his face was covered with more of the thickened, ring-shaped sores; his left fingers were totally useless, limp and gray-skinned. He had watched as Percy used his dead hand as a wedge for his good one at the kilns and had seen the skin break and bleed, but detected no sign of pain or sensation from Percy.

And from the shuffling gait of the man, Christian now suspected that Percy's feet were suffering too.

In the darkness, Christian's eyes dilated, and he felt cold.

One of mankind's oldest diseases—gone from his world of 2072, but festering with fecund morbidity in these latitudes of the nineteenth century, a bacillus nurtured in heat and filth and tropical humidity.

He had read of the lazarettos of the Middle Ages, of the ones required to sound a rattle to announce their presence to others.

Of those who were pronounced Unclean.

Of leprosy.

The sweat chilled him.

He began to shake.

28 November, 1835

Eating his breakfast slops from his bowl with his good hand, Percy became aware of Dalton watching him. He squinted at the man who was his friend, focusing the one eye that still opened cleanly.

Under his breath, Dalton spoke. "What'll happen to you when they find out?"

Percy fed more pasty mush between his almost paralyzed lips, swallowing it noisily, without concession to the effects of the sounds on others. He was beyond that. "They'll find a way to kill me. Feed me to the sharks." He glanced furtively about him. "I think they're beginning to suspect." He continued to feed.

"What can you do?"

Percy stopped chewing, looking at him in surprise. "Nothing," he said.

"Can I help?"

Christian saw what he thought was a smile. "No," Percy said.

They ate in silence for a time. Then Percy spoke. "Thanks," he said.

The word bit at Christian's heart.

2 December, 1835

Christian watched in the darkness of their sleeping quarters as Percy pulled his shoe and stocking from his foot with his good hand. Even though he had his back to Christian, the angle was such that a shaft of moonlight lit the corner of the room with a spectral silvering.

In the pale white light, Christian saw that two of the man's toes were missing. From the condition of the others, he would lose them shortly as well.

He could think of nothing to say.

11 December, 1835

"I'm going to escape," Percy said.

Christian looked at him.

"It's just about over."

Christian rolled his head back and watched the clouds race across the bright, blue sky. The wind brought the salt sea to his nostrils, mixed with the scent of pine. Gulls squawked and reeled above.

For you, he thought. Yes. Over.

And then the salt of his own tears stung his eyes, as once again he tried to adjust to the moral lassitude toward human life that was everywhere around him, and as once again, he failed.

23 December, 1835

"You there!"

Christian and the others looked up at the guard who had shouted. The two remaining guards raised their rifles.

Percy Teversham was shuffling away from the group that had been loading the lime onto the barge.

"Stop!"

He was heading for the water's edge. There was nothing ahead of him but the sea, vast and shining in the morning sun.

Christian and the others watched in silence, their mouths set grimly.

The guard raised his rifle. "Halt, you bloody fool!"

Percy plodded forward without looking back.

Christian watched him, frail and miniature against the swelling sea. *I'm going to escape,* he had said. *It's just about over.*

They all knew.

The guard adjusted the rifle in the crook of his arm and sighted on the prisoner.

Percy Teversham's feet touched the water and he continued to wade in.

They watched.

The guard squeezed the trigger. The sound was a slap in the face. The impact pitched Percy forward into the oncoming wave where he floated, face down, and was washed back toward the rest of them.

No one moved.

The guard lowered his rifle. "Jesus," he muttered.

The body rolled on the pebbly strand with the motion of the sea.

Two days later, Christmas was celebrated with an extra portion of mush at dinner. But the next eight months of 1836 crawled by with agonizing slowness on Norfolk.

VI

We can, if we so choose, do virtually anything: arid lands will become fertile; terrible diseases will be cured by genetic engineering; touring other planets will become routine; we may even come to understand how the human mind works!

— Richard E. Leakey, *Origins*

His soul swooned slowly as he heard the snow falling faintly through the universe and faintly falling, like the descent of their last end, upon all the living and the dead.

— James Joyce, "The Dead"

The rainbow comes and goes.

— Wordsworth, "Intimations of Immortality"

IV

44

TORONTO, CANADA

12 March, 2073

Liana heard the wail of life in the midst of pain.

Then, gently, the baby was placed for a moment on her stomach, smearing the blood and fluids from her own body on her skin.

"It's a boy, Mrs. Christian."

Her hands touched him, shaking. Yes, she thought. A boy. Fletcher. Fletcher Christian V.

And the tears that came were the same mixture of joy and grief that always came when she thought of the gift of the child and the loss of his father. Life would not allow happiness without sorrow over the long run.

But she had her memories. And she remembered the nights alone with Fletcher in Lima, their last times together, the wind from the Andes singing in the night as they embraced.

August, she thought. We try again in August. Five months from now.

She would return to Cuzco, to Huascar, to the site of the transmission, and hope for a miracle.

Then she glanced at the wrinkled, wailing child, listened to his vibrant meeting with life, and amended her thought slightly. Hope for *another* miracle, she thought.

* * **45** * *

MURUROA ATOLL

15 August, 1973

Obscured by the rains and black clouds, *La Dunkerquoise* was barely visible as dawn broke.

"How far?" asked Nigel.

"A mile. Maybe more," said McTaggart.

"And how far from the actual atoll?"

"Fourteen miles."

The wind was dying. *Greenpeace III's* second voyage into the shadow of the French bomb had been launched with less fanfare, less enthusiasm, and more misgivings. Besides McTaggart, only Nigel Ingram was a hold-over from the previous year. The rest of the crew consisted of two women, Ann-Marie Horne and Mary Lornie.

Female companionship had its own obvious benefits, thought McTaggart. He also hoped that it might deter the French plans in a way that an all-male crew had not. Gallic chivalry. Public sentiment. Women would present a different problem. And they did.

Then he saw it.

"There."

"What?"

McTaggart pointed.

The balloon rose above the horizon. The other three lifted binoculars. It swayed in the wind.

No one said anything.

Later, they watched as a high-speed cutter—a vedette—rendezvoused with the minesweeper *La Dunkerquoise*. Then a third ship appeared. Eventually, they all headed toward the small crew who were posing such a nuisance—this flea in the ear of the French destiny.

The four of them could only wait.

But they could also be afraid.

When they were boarded, they expected that things would be unpleasant. It was conceivable that things might be said, that threats would be bandied. But in their wildest fantasies they had not imagined that they were about to be physically set upon. In this sense, the presence of the women did make a difference—a vital one. For as the truncheons came down on McTaggart's head, neck, back, and kidneys, as they rained down upon Nigel's face and head, the women were merely bruised and manhandled. As Nigel was being kicked in the groin and ribs, and as McTaggart was taking the blow that would permanently damage his right eye, Ann-Marie was photographing the entire episode with her Nikon.

When one of the men saw her, she fled down the hatch below deck, extracted the film, and hid it in her vagina. The cameras and film that were subsequently thrown overboard were not what they sought to be rid of, and the damaging evidence eventually surfaced in the world's press to contradict the official French version of what had transpired that day.

All of this increased the pressure, and, in time, France ceded to it, in degrees. But always with typical French resistance. The tests went underground at Mururoa.

But not yet.

Not yet.

There was one more.

The next day.

The balloon still hovered, swayed. The sea quieted. In the past, in the future, ghosts swirled. Waiting.

· · 46 · ·

PITCAIRN ISLAND
15 August, 1973

"Mornin', Bran. Mornin' Lisa."

"Mornin', Edward."

They strode past the Co-op in the square, nodding to the others sitting on the veranda. The sign in the left window read "Disinfectant 40¢/pt. Please bring empty bottle." The announcement in the right window said, "22 pounds of butter left." It had not changed in three weeks.

The cries of children playing around and on the twelve-foot stern-anchor from the *Bounty* in the square caused Bran to watch with amusement. Pulled from Bounty Bay, it was one of only two pieces of *Bounty*ana on the island; the other, the *Bounty* bible, was not nearly as interesting to the children, for they could not swing on it, nor climb it.

Bran eyed its straight V flukes, and thought of the past that was only a year ago for him. The children were now pelting each other with ripe mangoes. There was no past for them.

"Mornin', Bran. Lisa."

"Mornin' Agnes."

They walked on down the dirt path, heading home. Bran liked being accepted. He had come to like his life very much. He placed his hand on

Lisa's shoulder.

And then they were within view of their house.

The walls—wood from sea flotsam, island timber, plywood from tea chests—sagged precariously, both from its basic unsuitability and from the infestation of the termites. A thick green moss coated it on the seaside. A shimmer of heat rose from the patched and rusted corrugated iron roof, even this early in the morning. Jars, bottles, drums, and toys littered the front of the dwelling.

They stopped to scrape the heavy Pitcairn mud from the soles and sides of their bare feet on the strip of iron set in wooden uprights by the front door. Frangipani and hibiscus blossoms flowered the air sweetly. Bran inhaled it with satisfaction.

Lisa's mother opened the door for them, the baby in her arms. Bran took his four-month-old son from her and held him aloft, a great Irish smile spreading across his wide face. Then he glanced at Lisa, and knew that there would never be any accounting for his luck.

If Da could only see me now.

Held at arm's length above his father, Fletcher Christian IV's great-grandfather cooed and chortled with delight in the morning light that brightened the room.

At Mururoa, the balloon hovered, the sea quieted.

On Norfolk, Christian rolled over, squinting against the morning sun, closing his eyes against the numbing pain that had become his life.

Ghosts swirled.

47

CUZCO, PERU
16 August, 2073

Faiths, like Empires, differ.

Some grow out of the dirt and cruel realities of the soil; some are the natural fruits of ancient and sophisticated cultures, the blossoms of traditions beyond memory; some are the storms that arise from the mind of a single, purposeful individual, a charismatic catalyst for the lightning that flashes everywhere without focus; some build like the rainwater in a cistern, the level dropping and rising, until the inevitable flood.

The New Inca faith, and the New Inca Empire, were all of these.

Huascar was the lightning rod.

They had waited more than a year. It was time.

Haucaypata Square.

Again.

But the differences were many.

This time, Huascar stood alone on the *usno* . This time the mood was more solemn, with less anticipation. Everyone sensed the degree of desperation that prevailed behind the scenes to have culminated in this moment.

Huascar had not attempted to utilize his gift since he had lost Fletcher

Christian IV in the void. Many said that he could no longer do it. Others said that he was afraid. Still others, with more insight, felt that he had lost some of the heart to continue, and they were closer to the truth.

Nevertheless, they had come to witness. The media were stacked three deep along the rooftops of the royal residences that surrounded the square. And in a specially allocated window in the Suntur Huasi, the elegant circular tower affronting Quishuarcancha, Huascar could see Liana and the boy—Christian's infant son—motionless. Waiting.

The moon was up.

The golden sun-pendant on Huascar's chest flashed in the sea of torchlight. He raised his hands. The crowd was hushed. It was beginning.

The fire blazed anew in Huascar's eyes, energized by the event. He was lost to the outside world. He had forfeited this man to the gods, and now he prayed that they would return him. But he was not sure. A new humility had settled on him, balancing the hubris.

"Hear me. Where are thou? Within? Without? In shadow? In cloud? Light the way through the funnel of Time, to our past, to our memory, to our destiny. Hear me. Respond. Be our guide."

The wind sprang up. The sand eddied.

"Oh memory, oh loss, within, without. Help us. Return him. Through Time."

Huascar felt himself being used. He was a vessel, a tool. The rivers of the Empire flowed through his soul, flooding him with the remnants of millions of lives, all awash in a cataract that arced into the past, leaving a rainbow of human joy and misery to the dawn of time. He shivered as the chords of human experience sounded their awesome music in his heart, and he understood that he, too, was about to join the rainbow of humanity and flow down Time's river.

Back.

To his final resting place.

He understood.

The moon flowed over him, liquid silver, melting him into the shadow of the past.

Before the eyes of the world, before the startled gaze of Liana and the uncomprehending eyes of Fletcher Christian V, Huascar faded to his destiny.

Under the starlit night, the *usno* was empty.

Huascar was gone.

Into the void.

The mushroom cloud blossomed in his mind.

* * 48 * *

MURUROA ATOLL

16 August, 1973

It rose in a seething column of fire and white light above the sea, a geyser of twisted power and shattered matter, piercing the clouds and boiling over, blinding beyond imagining. Then the rainbow colors began to glow in the atomic dust, and the cloud spread across the horizon, only to be punctured by yet another column of unleashed energy, casting unholy luminescence along the undersides of higher cumulostratus.

The wind and the noise followed.

For hours, in every direction.

And still it rolled on, unfolding like a giant flower, its invisible spores borne away on the updrafts and downwinds. The blast that would change everything.

Ghosts swirled.

49

Bran Michael Dalton stirred restlessly in his sleep. The sea that had gird-ed Pitcairn with its perpetual collar of white foam since the island had erupted from the vastest of Earth's oceans millions of years ago was strangely silent that night. In his sleep, Bran saw the hull of English oak wrapped in copper, saw the sweep of sails, white as snow against the blue of sky and water, and listened to His Majesty's armed transport *Bounty* cut through the lagoons of seas he had never known. And he heard the music of Michael Byrne, the half-blind fiddler who had signed on with William Bligh to entertain the crew His tunes ached with a melancholy that spoke of yearnings beyond the high seas.

Then he sensed, even in the depths of sleep, the presence that had vis-ited him only once before. He saw its mushroom shape, felt its power, was brushed by its awakening.

And he continued to dream of things that he could not possibly know.

But the power did not take him this time.

Instead, he felt it pass over him, like a wind, making him tremble.

By his side, Lisa shifted restlessly; in the corner of the room, the baby cried once, then was silent.

* * * * *

On Norfolk, Fletcher Christian IV felt the wind spring up somewhere inside him. In the darkness he opened his eyes. It was back.

The shape.

The power.

Something pulled from within his soul and he felt himself lifted into the gyre that would draw him from his body. Fear and hope: they stayed together, arms entwined, as he began to evaporate, began to join the power, whatever it was, wherever it would take him.

In his bed, Joseph Anderson stirred and turned.

Rebecca Anderson awoke suddenly, sat up, listened. But she heard nothing.

Fletcher Christian IV disappeared.

* * * * *

Huascar sailed the Time currents, his mind like glass, a prism through which everything passed before irradiating to infinity. And he saw everything.

His destiny.

His death.

The shape of everything, past and future.

His own power, the shattered atom, the Andean gods, the meteor shower, a ship on the high seas, men of courage and cowardice, women of insight and beauty, children for the infinite, awesome future. The flood of images cascaded through whatever was left of his mind, whatever synthesized such an array of seemingly disparate particles.

Losing Fletcher Christian IV, he understood now, was inevitable.

He arced through the void, drowning in his own knowledge, thankful for the glimpse.

* * * * *

Everything changed. Again.

* * * * *

When Percy Teversham awoke the next morning and glanced at the corpse of the man next to him, a fly buzzed in his brain. Something was awry, but he could not place it. His friend, Bran Michael Dalton, who slept beside him, was dead.

But every time he stared at the man's cream-colored robe, at the ornate golden sun-pendant hanging on his chest, at the white hair strewn with brilliant red feathers, he felt as if some small piece of information had been misplaced.

There was some puzzlement over the man's dress, but it quickly faded.

The fly buzzed in everyone's brain a great deal that day.

And as Percy lifted his friend's sun-pendant aloft in his left hand, which was as strong and healthy as his right one, and stared at it with both of his eyes, which were both keen and unencumbered by any growth or malignancy, he felt the sadness that any man would feel at the loss of a friend.

But he knew that he would survive.

He would leave Norfolk, get back to England, see his brother Will.

He *knew* it.

And it was true.

His fingers caressed the pendant, and he thought he could feel the warmth of the sun in its startling gold.

Dalton's sudden aging and his unusual garb and grooming stumped everyone. And every time they thought about it, they sensed an irretrievable piece of the puzzle missing, as though a single page in an enormous book had been turned without their knowledge.

The hands of Time shifted infinitesimally, erasing with them, as always, memories.

From different vantage points, Major Joseph Anderson, his daughter Rebecca, and Percy Teversham watched as a small boat rowed out to sea with the body in a pine box. They saw the men open the box and hoist the body out. They watched as the body was dropped into the sea.

Joseph Anderson thought of establishing a hospital on the island, and wondered where the idea had come from.

Rebecca turned from her window and went back to her sewing.

Percy lustily inhaled the salt air of the morning.

50

Christian was pulled back into the void that had brought him to Norfolk, a place without describable dimensions, a place of darkness and light. Even his body lacked form; there was only his consciousness, spinning with the release that made escape from physical chains seem an insignificant thing. He soared along the channel of Time, a great mythical bird, free.

But he knew that he was not headed home.

Behind him was the mushroom presence, its great, impossible wind hurling him back across the centuries.

Farther into the past.

There would be no more Norfolk. But, he understood, there would be no more Liana, either.

Back.

Time had taken him again.

Like a leaf in a cosmic storm, he was swept along, even farther back, impossibly far back.

There seemed to be no stopping this time, no point of destination. The centuries ticked by like dreams. The Crusades, the Eastern dynasties; the savage hordes of Europe; tribes roaming the deserts of Africa, the Roman armies; the pyramids, Babylon. He sensed it all, all passing in reverse.

And then it sped up. He was sailing backwards at an accelerated rate, not just centuries lapsing, but epochs. Glaciers came and went; species rose and fell. Man shrank into hunched bipedal gatherings.

And then Man disappeared.

The dinosaurs.

And they too shrank to nothing.

And then he understood.

He saw his destiny.

The earth was lifeless. No continents existed. Islands. It was all islands, poking volcanic heads above bleak, vast, dark seas. Lightning lit the skies.

He slowed down.

He saw the meteorite shower. It fell for months, years, in the dark seas, on the sterile islands, pelting the earth with carbonaceous chondrites.

Cosmic debris.

The meteorites rained on the planet for generations, each one containing some measure of amino acids, some measure of carboxylic acids, some measure of the chemical origins of Life.

Nor could he escape the corollaries of what he was seeing. Meteorites were not a phenomenon exclusive to the earth. They rained down on planets in every solar system, showering life upon a billion billion worlds, sowing seeds among the infinite oceans of stars and galaxies.

The Universe was in the business of making Life.

But this world, this planet, the earth, was to be his.

He was the seed that would be the future. The Idea of Man had to be as perfect as possible. In the Rainbow Arc of Time, Man was a stream whose source was himself, and Fletcher Christian IV would re-invent the world at its origin, its heart. He would be the Creator.

The mutiny on the Bounty, the search for Eden that ended on Pitcairn, the courage of a few who sailed to Mururoa, the need to heal on Norfolk, the rise of the New Incas in Peru, the soaring trajectory along the Tropic of Capricorn: all rose as colored flares in the storm of suns that exploded like crystals in his mind.

He was following the rainbow to its end.

There were beginnings and there were Beginnings.

He was still travelling back, drifting down the Time stream, on the grandest adventure imaginable.

To the Beginning.

26 June, 2103

High in the Andes, near the ruins of Ingapirca, on the earth's spine, the wind sang through the ancient corridors, rippling the pools that had gathered in the worn stone crevices, shimmering the miniature rainbows where no one would see them.

In Cuzco, Liana Christian looked at the young man, his face and bearing so like that of his father.

"I have to go," said Fletcher Christian V. "I have to try."

She nodded. "I know."

He was thirty years old, in his prime.

"Huascar's disciples have succeeded. They can finally do it." He stared into his mother's eyes, seeing the beauty that his father must have seen. "I have no choice."

She understood.

"Wherever it takes me."

She watched his face, haunted by the circle of future and past, alive with a destiny she could not grasp.

He touched his mother's face with his right hand, the light twisting in the red stone of his ring.

"I must find my father."

A F T E R W O R D

by Robert J. Sawyer

As Terence M. Green says in his introduction to this book, in 1992, McClelland and Stewart, Canada's largest publisher, tried a grand experiment: they published a science-fiction novel. Yes, sure, they'd done that before—Margaret Atwood's *The Handmaid's Tale* and Hugh MacLennan's *Voices in Time* come to mind. But, for those books, they hid the fact that they were publishing SF; indeed, they did everything they could to distance them from the genre.

But when they acquired *Children of the Rainbow*, they also acquired Terry Green's track record of great success in science fiction. His brilliant short work in the American digests *Asimov's Science Fiction* and *The Magazine of Fantasy and Science Fiction* had been collected in *The Woman Who is the Midnight Wind* (Pottersfield, 1987), which Orson Scott Card had hailed "as a milestone for all of us." And Green's much-lauded first novel, *Barking Dogs* (St. Martin's Press, 1988), was, according to *Locus*, the US trade journal of the SF field, "not to be missed."

And so, M&S decided to present *Children of the Rainbow* as SF, a first for them; they even solicited a cover blurb from me, which I stand by to this day: "If H.G. Wells could have hand-picked a successor to use time travel as a literary device, he'd have chosen Terence M. Green." But despite their best intentions, M&S did about as good a job of presenting this science-fiction novel as, say, a publisher of waltzes might do with an album of rock 'n' roll.

The intent had been to appeal to both SF fans and mainstream readers; the resulting package appealed to neither—even though there was indeed much crossover potential. As Green said in an interview back then, "This story is about two people displaced in space and time. You don't have to be a science-fiction reader to appreciate that. We're all displaced in one way or another. One of my characters is displaced happily; the other, miserably. In the novel, they're displaced through time by a nuclear blast. Metaphorically, everyone at some point in their life encounters a nuclear blast: the death of a loved one, the breakup of a long-standing relationship, the loss of a job. You're displaced, but you cope somehow. You go on. That's the psychological realism of the book."

Of course, in a decade and a half, a writer can have second thoughts; when I acquired reprint rights to *Children of the Rainbow*, I asked Terry if he wanted to revise the text; this new edition, which we've given a more fitting title, *Sailing Time's Ocean*, is the result.

A lot has happened to Terry in the years since, all of it good. He's retired from teaching English; published four more first-rate novels with Tor, the world's largest SF publisher; and joined the creative-writing faculty of the University of Western Ontario. He's married for a second time, to the wonderful Merle Casci; his sons from his first marriage have grown up; and, in his fifties, he's become a father again, to young Daniel.

Still, to those of us who knew Terry back when the first edition of this book appeared (he and I have been friends for almost twenty-five years now), it was no surprise that in the acknowledgments he listed "with real fondness" the apartment on Heath Street East in Toronto where he put his own life back together after one of his own personal nuclear blasts: the break-up of his first marriage. His next novel after *Children of the Rainbow*, the World Fantasy Award finalist *Shadow of Ashland*, likewise struggled with the aftermath of another such blast: the death of his mother.

"It wasn't until I started dealing with these sorts of things that my writing hit its power," Terry said at the time. "Up until then, I'd been writing stuff. Now I incorporate painful life experience. That turned out to be my voice—the horrors of my life. A writer has to deal with what's really important, with what really moves you."

Perhaps the best assessment Green's work came from the late, great Judith Merril, the principal American editor during SF's literary "New Wave" movement of the 1960s:

Terry Green wants to know what love is all about—how it happens, why it happens, what it does for/to people who love or are loved. Using the uniquely flexible 'special effects' of science fantasy—dislocations in space and time, alien cultures, trick technology, outright magic—he distances / magnifies / highlights / contrasts the mechanisms and meanings of these most familiar and least understood of all human experiences.

In a similar vein, M.T. Kelly, winner of the Governor General's Award for fiction, said that the book you're now holding is "written with passion and love. Its great humanity and religious sense are as clear as the Pacific."

All the same, for one so fascinated by love, Green is often characterized as being an angry writer. It's that anger that drove his first novel, *Barking Dogs*, in which police officer Mitch Helwig of Toronto's finest goes on a vigilante spree, cleaning up the city's streets. He's armed with a hand laser and the Barking Dog of the title, an infallible lie detector that lets him play judge and jury to the scum making the city Green grew up in unsafe. It's no mere coincidence that Green dedicated *Barking Dogs* to his two sons, Conor and Owen: his anger is that of a father enraged by what's happening to the world his beloved children will grow up in.

Likewise, this passage from *Sailing Time's Ocean* is quintessential Green. Here, Major Anderson, the commandant of the Norfolk Island penal colony in 1835, faces a man from the future who has taken the place of one of his prisoners:

Anderson studied the man. "I will tell you this: I am outraged that you are somehow involved in something that has to do with my family. May

God help you if you step in where you have absolutely no business. I will forget that I am a soldier, an officer, and will let you know the full measure of my wrath as a husband and father."

Green does write with anger, and with conviction, but it is all driven by the love Judith Merril and M.T. Kelly cite. For Terence M. Green, the limitless vistas of space and time are simply metaphor. More than anything else, he's writing about family.

Terry and this book have both sailed time's ocean since the first edition appeared—and he and I hope you enjoyed the journey you've just completed. This story has stuck in my mind for fifteen years now. I rather suspect it'll do the same for you.

BOOK CLUB GUIDE

RECOMMENDED FURTHER READING

Research should be both education and joy. This was certainly the case with this novel. Readers might be interested in sampling the stories and the wealth of information available in the following books… and perhaps using them as the basis for further discussions.

Robinson Crusoe (1719), by Daniel Defoe
The Bounty Trilogy, by Charles Nordhoff and James Hall:
* *Mutiny on the Bounty* (1932)
* *Men Against the Sea* (1933)
* *Pitcairn's Island* (1934)
Pitcairn: Children of Mutiny (1973), by Ian M. Ball
Alexander Maconochie of Norfolk Island (1958), by
    John Vincent Barry
Lords of Cuzco (1967), by Burr Cartwright Brundage
Greenpeace III: Journey into the Bomb (1978), by
    David McTaggart with Robert Hunter

AREAS FOR DISCUSSION AND EXPLORATION:

- Penal Institutions: Rehabilitation? Punishment? Isolation? Uses for Society?

- Use, abuse, misuse of natural resources (a) in the novel (b) today.

- The novel focuses on the power of ancestry in our lives. Create a personal family tree, reflecting upon the interplay of genetics and environment that you find there.

- Cuzco, Haucaypata Square and Ingapirca appear as "sacred places" in the novel. List some other "sacred places" and discuss their importance in history. Have you ever made a "pilgrimage" to such a site? If so, why? What was your reaction?

- In the novel, Bran Michael Dalton gets a "second chance" when he finds himself on Pitcairn Island. Have you ever been afforded a "second chance" in a significant area of your life? Explain. Were you able to take advantage of the opportunity?

- Pitcairn Island stands as a textbook case for a culture formed "in isolation." What is its importance for us today, if any?

- If you were Fletcher Christian IV, how would you convince Joseph Anderson that you were indeed "from the future?"

- To paraphrase Robert Burns, "the best laid plans of mice and men often go astray." John Steinbeck was insightful enough to seize upon the gist of this adage as the title for one of his finest novels (*Of Mice and Men*).

  In *Sailing Time's Ocean*, how does this aphorism apply to most of the characters?

(Does it have relevance to your own life?)

- Using the internet and any other sources, find out (and discuss) what happened to David McTaggart between 1972 and his death in 2001.

- In the novel's *Afterword*, Green is quoted discussing the metaphor of the "nuclear blast" as a commonplace in everyone's life. What have been your own personal "nuclear blasts?" How did they change you or the direction of your life?

ABOUT THE AUTHOR

Terence M. Green, the author of seven previous books (six novels and a collection of short stories), has been profiled in such places as *Canadian Who's Who*, *Contemporary Authors* and *The Oxford Companion to Canadian Literature*. Praised as widely as The New York Times, The San Francisco Chronicle, The Globe and Mail, The Toronto Star, The Ottawa Citizen and The Atlantic Constitution, 1996's *Shadow of Ashland* and 1999's *A Witness to Life* were both World Fantasy Award Finalists for Best Novel. As well, he is a five-time finalist for Canada's Prix Aurora Award.

Shadow of Ashland, selected as a "Top Fiction Pick of the Year" by The Edmonton Journal (1997) and "The Book You Have to Read" by Entertainment Weekly (2003), was broadcast on CBC Radio's "Between the Covers" – airing on more than four hundred stations nation-wide, over two weeks in the fall of 2002.

Recipient of a total of nine Canada Council, Ontario Arts Council and Toronto Arts Council grants for fiction, twice a participant in the Harbourfront International Festival of Authors, he has conducted writing workshops and given talks widely — from London, England to Florida to the Yukon.

Until his retirement in 1999, Green taught English in Ontario secondary schools over a thirty-one year span. Since then, he has written full time, had both short and long work broadcast on CBC Radio, been keynote speaker at the Sixty-Second annual University of Oklahoma Writers Conference, instructed at the Yukon Writers Retreat (with the support of the Yukon Arts Fund), served (under a Canada Council for the Arts grant) as Writer-in-Residence at Mohawk College in Hamilton, Ontario (2003-2004), acted as juror for the 3rd annual Sunburst Award (2003) and been a full-time stay-at-home Dad. In 2005, he joined the Faculty of Arts and Humanities at The University of Western Ontario, where he is currently a lecturer in creative writing.

He holds an M.A. in Anglo-Irish Literature and Drama from University College, Dublin, and B.A. (English) and B.Ed. degrees from the University of Toronto. During a sabbatical year from teaching, he studied Computers and Writing at the Harvard Graduate School of Education. His shorter work has appeared everywhere from The Magazine of Fantasy and Science Fiction to The Globe and Mail.

Born in Toronto in 1947, he and his wife and three sons still call it home. For more information, you are invited to visit his web site at *tmgreen.com.*

BOOKS BY
TERENCE M. GREEN

The Woman Who is the Midnight Wind
Barking Dogs
Blue Limbo
Shadow of Ashland
A Witness to Life
St. Patrick's Bed
Sailing Time's Ocean

BOOKS UNDER THE
ROBERT J. SAWYER BOOKS IMPRINT

Letters From the Flesh by Marcos Donnelly
Getting Near the End by Andrew Weiner
The Engine of Recall by Karl Schroeder
Rogue Harvest by Danita Maslan
A Small and Remarkable Life by Nick DiChario
Sailing Time's Ocean by Terence M. Green